"That's going to be a hard one to top," Glen said. "But whose turn is it next?" Glen looked around, then squinted at me. I turned away and stared at a spot on the carpet, hoping he'd move on. No such luck. "Next victim, Jessica Carvelli. Truth or Dare?"

My face felt hot as I pushed up and sat on the dresser again. "I'm not letting anyone see my underwear."

"Big surprise," Erin said. "She's going to pick Truth." She turned to Amber's group. "Jessica always picks Truth. She's not the daring type."

Thanks a lot, Erin, I thought.

"No kidding," said one of Amber's friends.

I blinked. The comment came from a guy I barely knew. I crossed my arms, a little surprised. Did *everyone* think I was boring? I was getting a little tired of hearing how I needed to loosen up, be more fun, and ignore my schoolwork. If people thought I was a geek, they really didn't know me. I loved having fun. Fun was my middle name. Really.

Lifting my chin, I shot Erin a willful look and answered, "I pick Dare."

9

TURNING
seventeen

Just Trust Me

by Rosalind Noonan

A PARACHUTE PRESS BOOK

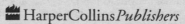 HarperCollins*Publishers*

Created and produced by
PARACHUTE PUBLISHING, L.L.C.
156 Fifth Avenue, Suite 302
New York, NY 10010

Published by
HarperCollins *Publishers*
1350 Avenue of the Americas
New York, NY 10019

First HarperCollins *Publishers* printing, May 2001

HarperCollins® and 📖®
are trademarks of HarperCollins *Publishers* Inc.

Library of Congress Catalog Card Number: 00-111222
ISBN 0-06-447343-0

Printed in the U.S.A.

10 9 8 7 6 5 4 3 2 1

Design by AFF Design
Cover photos by Anna Palma

Just Trust Me

Chapter 1

Kerri

"It's Senior Trip!" I told my three best friends, Jessica Carvelli, Erin Yamada, and Maya Greer, as we entered Banana Republic in the mall on Saturday. As if just saying the words would somehow invoke world peace or something. Okay, maybe not world peace. But just knowing that I'd be getting away for a week of fun in Chicago, starting Monday, made all my problems seem a little smaller.

"I have to confess," I added. "It's coming at exactly the right time for Matt and me. Not that I don't want to party with you guys, but I need this week with my boyfriend. With his band and my cheerleading and all our papers and tests and things, it's been really hard to connect with him lately."

There was an awkward silence, punctuated only by the bleep of the cash register in the distance. Erin turned away from a mirror, where

1

she was trying on a tiger-print scarf. Jessica and Maya didn't look up from the stack of jeans in front of them, but I felt their concern. I knew that my friends weren't exactly sure what was going on with Matt Fowler and me these days. One minute we were soul mates, and the next minute we were fighting over something trivial.

"Are you worried?" Maya asked me. "I mean, about your relationship?"

"After all we've been through?" I said, trying to sound casual, as though I thought Maya's question was ridiculous. Inside, I wasn't so sure it was.

"Kerri's right," Jessica said. "Think about it. How many relationships can survive an ex-girlfriend like Donna Cantreal?"

"You're being too nice," Erin said. She tucked the scarf back onto the rack. "That girl is a stalker with a capital 'S.'"

I leaned on a table with some pastel sweaters on it and pressed my fingernails into my palms. It still bothered me to think about Donna, even though she wasn't supposed to call me or come near me. My mother had made sure of that, insisting that we get a restraining order against her.

I admit, when Donna first showed up at Maya's track meet a few weeks ago, I felt a little jealous. I mean, she just ran up to Matt and threw her arms around him as if they were the last two survivors on an island. Right in front of everybody.

Things just got weirder from there. First, Donna kept saying that she and Matt were still dating. Then she blamed me for stealing Matt away from her—when they had broken up way before Matt and I started going out.

Then things became scary. Donna started hanging out in front of my apartment, calling me at all hours, popping up at my job at Bernie's Bagels and at the one modeling gig I had at the mall. She even slashed the tires of my car. And when stalking me didn't win Matt back, she tried to mow me down with her Jetta.

That was when my mom went with me to get the court order.

Donna denied that she did it on purpose. She told the police that her car swerved toward my friends and me when she was dialing her cell phone. She said it was an accident.

But I didn't believe her. I still don't.

"I am so glad she's out of the picture," Maya said, slipping an arm around my shoulders.

Jessica nodded. "I never thought she'd go that far. Boy, did I misjudge her."

"We all did," I said. "But the important thing is that she's gone, and Matt and I are still together. . . .

I just miss the way things used to be between us . . . so fun and easy."

Jessica sighed as she slid her hands into a pair of chocolate-brown cashmere gloves. "I remember what it was like to have a boyfriend . . . I think." She pulled off the gloves and tossed them back on the counter. "You know, it feels like I've been without a guy for years, even though it's been only a few months." Jessica had broken up with Alex McKay, her boyfriend of two years, at the start of senior year.

"You'll find someone," Maya said reassuringly. "Maybe in Chicago?"

"Nope. G.U." Erin's ponytails jiggled as she shook her head. "Geographically Undesirable."

"Forget about finding a guy in Chicago," I said. "We are just going to hang out and have fun. Matt says they have really cool jazz clubs there."

"I'm looking forward to spending a big chunk of time with Luke *without* my dad looking over our shoulders," Maya said. "Plus Chicago's got great shopping."

"And the Art Institute," Erin said. "I could just move into a back room at that place." Erin slid a red sweater over her shoulders, tied it there, and made a face in the mirror.

"And the *Tribune*," Jessica added. "I heard

we're going to tour the place to see behind the scenes at a major newspaper."

I smiled. Leave it to Jess, the writer, to get psyched about a newspaper tour. "This is going to be a landmark in our senior year," I told my friends. "A whole week without parents."

"And how about hanging at the hotel with the boyfriends?" Erin said. "How cool is that?"

"Way cool for you guys," Jessica said, moving over to a rack of hats. "I'm going to be the seventh wheel."

"Oh, right," I said. "Like that would *ever* be true." I pulled a green cap off the rack and handed it to her. "Here, try this on."

Jessica plunked the hat on her head and stared into the mirror. Her superlong dark hair streamed out from the sides. "Not my color," she muttered, and put back the hat.

"Hey!" Erin cried as I scanned the store, looking for the sale rack. "What about our Truth or Dare game? We left off with you, Kerri. What did you pick? A dare, right?"

I nodded, spotting a rust-colored sheepskin jacket. I took the hanger off the rack.

"That is so you, Kerri," Maya said.

And so out of my price range, I thought, when I got a glimpse of the price tag.

5

"Okay, I've got a dare for Kerri," Erin said, glancing at the display window at the front of the store. "Climb into the window and pretend you're a mannequin for thirty seconds."

I tossed back my hair, liking the idea. It would be fun seeing how shoppers would react.

"I don't think she should." Jessica frowned and glanced around. "What if she gets caught? We could get kicked out of the store."

"Big deal," Erin said. "This place is boring anyway. Their fashion is so . . . predictable."

I stared at Erin's orange-purple-and-red skirt and smiled. The girl was not exactly into muted colors. Erin was Asian American, with lively almond-shaped eyes, a great smile, and a definite wild streak.

"Besides," Maya added, "Kerri picked Dare, so she has to do it. We all did a dare. Well, everybody except Jess." She turned to her. "But don't worry. We'll get to you, Jessie girl."

Jess seemed to squirm a little. Okay, so she was the least adventurous of our group, but the thought of taking the dare made me smile. "I'll do it," I announced.

I glanced behind me to make sure none of the salespeople were nearby. Then I handed Maya my coat, slipped on the sheepskin jacket, and made my way to the display window.

I climbed onto the platform and struck a pose between two pale blue sweaters twisted around steel hangers with black pants rippled beneath them. Frozen in position, I stared through the window of Banana Republic out into the mall full of people and kids.

I tried to keep a serious expression on my face, but my friends were laughing so hard behind me that I couldn't help giggling with them. "Time?" I turned to Erin.

"Twenty-five seconds more," Erin called.

"Hurry up," Jessica whispered.

I put on my serious look and gazed out into the mall again. Two women on a bench were pointing at me, amused. A passing man crossed his eyes, trying to make me laugh.

I scanned the people on the main escalators. Going up was a blond woman with her crying two-year-old. Two guys I didn't recognize, wearing Westdale High jackets. Only one person was going down—a skinny man with a *really big* head.

"Ten seconds," Maya said.

Then I spotted another person on the down escalator. A girl with dark, bobbed hair. I felt an uneasiness in my stomach. She kind of looked like . . .

I shivered as the girl's pale blue eyes fixed onto mine.

"Donna," I breathed. She wasn't supposed to come within a hundred yards of me, yet here she was. She didn't seem to care about the restraining order.

My chest tightened as Donna was slowly transported down to the first floor. As she stared at me the whole time. As she stepped off the escalator . . .

"Time's up," Jessica said.

"Way to go, Ker!" Erin whooped.

I wanted to hop out of the display. To get away. But I couldn't even speak. My muscles felt dead and frozen as I watched Donna walk toward me.

Chapter 2

"**K**erri?" Maya leaned in and put her hand on my arm. "What's wrong?"

I pointed to the glass window, ready to let out a scream. But when Maya followed my gaze, Donna continued walking past the benches . . . off into the crowd.

"It's Donna," I said. Climbing out of the display window, I nearly collapsed onto the floor. My knees were shaking with fear, and I felt sick.

"I saw her," Maya replied. We stared through the window, watching out for Donna.

"Are you okay?" Jessica asked.

"Yeah," I lied. My knees were still quivering, and my throat felt tight. Jess slid back and studied me.

"What did she do?" Erin asked. "Did she say something?"

"No," I replied. "She just looked at me. Do you think I should call the police?"

Maya bit her lower lip. Slowly she reached into her bag and handed me her cell phone.

Erin peered through the glass, shaking her head. "She's gone. Maybe the whole thing was a fluke."

I flipped the phone open and paused. *Donna's allowed to shop at the mall,* I thought. *She just has to walk the other way when she sees me. And that's what she did.*

I closed the phone and gave it back to Maya. "Erin's probably right," I said, folding my arms to ward off another shiver.

After Mom got the court order, I honestly thought I'd never see Donna again. Maybe that was unrealistic. Seeing her now made me wonder if I'd always have to look twice before I took a step. I just hoped that one day I would truly feel safe again.

After Maya bought a sweater and Jessica got a black scarf, we headed out to the food court for a change of scene. As I dug into my raspberry frozen yogurt with walnuts, Erin told us about an old backpack she was decorating with lacquered pictures cut out from cereal boxes.

"I was going for funky, but it's turning out funny. There's a goofy rabbit and a bunch of bees and a teddy bear holding a honey wand," Erin said, scooping a bunch of chocolate chips off her triple chocolate yogurt. "I just hope it dries in time for me to bring it to Chicago."

"Ugh, what time is it, anyway?" Jessica checked her watch. "Almost four. I'd better bail."

"No, wait," I insisted, not wanting Jess to leave so soon. She was in a special program that allowed her to take college classes at the University of Wisconsin while she was still in high school. Even if she did have lots of schoolwork, she needed some time to kick back with her friends. Jess was so serious about her studies and projects. That's why I loved to corrupt her. Which was a challenge, since she was so incorruptible. "We didn't finish our Truth or Dare game."

"That's right," Maya said, pushing a strand of dark hair off her shoulder. "And isn't it your turn, Jess?"

Erin grinned, swallowing a mouthful of yogurt. "Your number's up, baby. Truth or Dare?"

"Okay, okay." Jess rolled her dark eyes as she leaned back in the chair. "Truth. Bring it on."

Erin frowned. "Why don't you ever pick Dare?" she asked. "Truth is so dull. . . . Come on, Jess. I've got a really good one for you."

"Yeah, and your mission is to totally humiliate me in the middle of the mall. I don't think so," Jess replied. "Truth."

"Hmm." I drummed my fingers on the table, trying to think of a question for her. "This is tough. I already know everything about you."

Maya licked her spoon, then pointed it at Jess. "I've got one. Who, in your experience, is the absolute best kisser?"

"Oh, please." Erin raked back her hair, revealing the raspberry highlights she'd touched up last week, while her parents were out of the house. "Easy answer. Everyone knows it's going to be Alex." Alex McKay, the love of Jess's life. At least until recently. Now she seemed to be really over him. But as far as Alex being the best kisser . . . I had my doubts.

"Guess again," Jessica said. "Alex had his talents, but we never got too far in the physical department."

"So . . ." Maya prodded. "What's your answer?"

I watched as Jessica folded her arms and smiled. "Scott Seifert."

"Ooh! The spoiler!" Erin said.

"So it's true what they say about those college guys," I teased Jess. Scott was a college student Jess had kind of gotten involved with while she was still seeing Alex.

"Scott was a great kisser," Jess said. She narrowed her dark eyes. "Can't trust him at all, but the guy had a kissing technique that made my knees melt."

Erin and Maya laughed. I just smiled at Jess, who grinned back with a mischievous look.

I sat back and spotted Matt coming up the escalator. Just seeing him made me smile a little. "Talk about melting knees," I said. "Here comes Matt."

"Which means I must be really late now," Jessica said, turning around to wave to Matt. "Hey, Matt. You missed all the excitement."

"Lucky you," I told Matt as he turned a chair around and straddled it. I didn't really want to go through the whole story about Donna again now.

"Really?" Matt picked a walnut from my sundae and popped it in his mouth. "Well, I've got some news that'll kick yours. Guess who's going to be performing in Chicago while we're there?"

"Limp Bizkit?" Erin said.

"*NSync?" Maya asked, her brown eyes lighting up.

"Duke Gaylord," Matt announced as if we should all jump up and cheer.

Maya and Jessica looked puzzled. "Who's he?" Maya asked.

Matt held up his hands as if he couldn't believe us. "He's just the greatest jazz guitarist alive. I'm going to go online to get tickets. Who's in?"

Silence. The girls were less than enthused.

"Jazz isn't really our thing," Erin told Matt.

"And I'm sure it's expensive," Jessica said, zipping up her jacket. "I've got to save my money for a few choice events on the trip."

Matt turned to Maya, who shook her head. "I've never even heard of the guy before this."

"You girls don't know what you're missing," Matt said. He reached for my hand and linked his fingers through mine. "Guess it's just going to be Kerri and me. But that's okay." He squeezed my hand.

"Fine with me," I said. Not that I knew anything about Duke Gaylord, but Matt seemed so psyched about the concert. And it would be one more chance for us to spend time alone together.

"Anyway," Jess said, standing up, "I was just leaving."

"Finish your yogurt," I insisted.

Jessica slung her backpack over one shoulder and took a giant bite of her sundae.

I waved my spoon at her. "Easy, Jess. You've got to give yourself a little time to live."

She swallowed and said, "Nope. That got cut from the schedule, along with time to breathe, think, and do my nails."

"We can give you a manicure tonight at the sleepover," Erin promised.

"Great. See you then." Jessica turned and nearly ran toward the north exit.

"We'd better get moving too," Erin said. "I mean, if you want to check out the sale at Old Navy. I hope they still have those sparkly T-shirts."

"Let's go," Maya said, picking up her chocolate shake. "See you tonight, Ker."

I waved good-bye, then pushed my melting yogurt across the table to Matt. It was obvious that they were leaving me alone to relay the Donna encounter to him. I just wished it had never happened and that I never had to think of her again.

"Whoa. Major storm front," Matt said, looking up from the frozen yogurt. "Who died?"

"It's not that bad," I said. "But I just saw Donna downstairs." He listened carefully as I told him everything, including where I was standing, where she was looking, which way she went—the whole enchilada. "Everyone is convinced it was just a chance meeting, but I don't know," I said. "She still freaks me out."

"Come here." Matt dropped the spoon into the yogurt dish and pulled his chair closer to mine. He slid an arm around my shoulders and leaned in so that his face was just inches away from mine. His blue eyes glimmered as he spoke. "You know, I think your friends are right. It sounds like a total coincidence. But this is so unfair to you. I can understand why you're upset."

Upset? I was crumbling inside. Tears began to form in my eyes, and I looked away, suddenly wanting to escape from the middle of the mall.

"Hey." Matt pressed his face to mine. "Don't cry. You're the sane one. Donna is the nutcase. A total Looney Toon."

I couldn't help but smile as I imagined a dazed Tweety Bird. I sniffed and wiped my eyes.

"That's better," Matt said, smoothing my hair over my shoulders. "Look, you know if she comes near you again on purpose she'll be locked up. So don't sweat it, okay?"

I nodded. "I just want her to leave me alone." I swiped at my eyes again and took a deep breath. "One more reason to go to Chicago. It'll be nice to put some distance between that girl and me. Like a few hundred miles."

"She can eat our dust," Matt said, grinning. "But you've got to get Donna out of your mind. Think about something else. Something positive." He put his fingers under my chin and lifted my face to his. "Think about us."

Sitting there, in the middle of the mall on a Saturday afternoon, I felt closer to Matt than I had in a long time. There was definitely something special between us. And this trip was just what we needed—a chance to get our relationship back on solid ground.

All around us were people moving, shopping, chasing their kids; Muzak playing, popcorn popping, escalators rolling. But as Matt kissed me, I felt as though we'd created our own universe within all the noise and commotion. For now, Matt's kiss was the center of my world—our world.

Jessica

However, the radio industry changed dramatically with the introduction of television broadcasting in 19

The unfinished sentence hung on my computer screen as I leafed through the textbook on my lap, trying to come up with the date.

I was supposed to be typing up my college paper on the evolution of the radio industry—just one of the many things I needed to finish before I left for Chicago.

I figured that I could type the paper tonight,

proofread it tomorrow, and then drop it in my professor's mailbox at the Student Union. Of course, that left me zero time for the ideas I needed to come up with for the online teen advice column I had just been hired to write.

I yawned. Why was I the only one running around like a remote-control robot? Other people had lots of schoolwork and job commitments. Maybe I took it all a little too seriously, but I couldn't help it. The professors at the university didn't mess around, and I hated getting a B in any class when I knew I could make an A. Colleges like New York University were going to see my grades. And NYU was where I wanted to be this time next year.

I looked at the phone, considering canceling out on the sleepover at Kerri's. The thought of finishing up my work and diving into bed early was tempting. Almost irresistible.

The phone rang, and I grabbed it, not wanting to annoy my parents.

"Hey, kiddo," said the voice on the phone. "What's up?"

It was my sister, Lisa, calling from college. Since she'd left for Marquette University we'd begun an extra-close long-distance relationship. I think she realized I wasn't such an annoying squirt, and I realized she gave great advice.

"I'm in the downhill stretch, trying to finish a paper," I said. "Mom's not here—grocery shopping, I think. Want her to call you back?"

"Nah, I was just checking in. What's your paper about?"

"Radio," I said. "And I've got to finish and hand it in before the bus leaves for senior trip Monday morning. Plus I've got stuff to do for my new job." I hoisted the stack of books from my lap to the desk and leaned back. "Tell me it gets easier when you're just going to college."

Lisa laughed. "I'll tell you that, if you don't mind a big fat lie."

"Your honesty is killing me."

"Sorry, but I won't sugar-coat it. Maybe things don't get harder in college, but they're certainly more complicated. Professors don't keep on top of you the way high school teachers do. If you fail, you're in it alone. It can be pretty cold."

I heard the beep signaling another call. "Someone else is calling. Do you want to hold?"

"No," Lisa said. "I'll call Mom later. Good luck with the paper."

"Thanks," I said, then quickly switched to the other call. It was Erin, calling from Maya's cell phone.

"You guys are still at the mall?" I asked.

"Just Maya and me. Kerri headed off for manual labor at Bernie's."

"Is Maya buying a new wardrobe for every day of the trip?" I joked, turning to the index in my textbook.

"Almost. But we've got an emergency assignment for you. We're in need of major munchies at Kerri's."

"Chips?" I squinted. "You call a snack run an emergency?"

I could hear Maya in the background, saying something about cheese and crackers and chocolate.

"What's a sleepover without junk food?" Erin asked.

"Pretty lame, but that's beside the point." I smelled a rat. There had to be another reason for them to call. "What's really up?"

There was a moment's hesitation. "Okay, you caught us. The munchies run was just an excuse to make sure you were coming."

"What?" I pushed my textbook aside, feeling a little guilty. Okay, I'd been thinking about bailing. But I wasn't about to admit it. "I told you I was coming," I said.

"Yeah, yeah, yeah," Erin said easily. "But you always say you're coming."

"Yeah, but—"

"No buts," Erin insisted. "We're worried about you, girl. If you don't watch out, pretty soon you'll be wearing a pair of glasses held together with tape, and it won't even faze you."

I was glad that we weren't having this conversation in person. It was embarrassing to hear that my friends thought I was turning into a nerd. "Gee, thanks," I said sarcastically.

"Don't take it personally," Erin said. "We know you work hard."

"But it is personal." I stood up and started pacing. "And a lot of people work hard. I mean, hard work alone doesn't put you on the Nerd of the Month list."

There was silence on the line. Was Erin actually at a loss for words?

Finally she said, "That's not really what I meant, Jess. You know we'll always love you, nerd or not. Not that you are. What I mean is . . ."

I sighed heavily in frustration. Erin was backpedaling. She must have realized she'd insulted me, and now the conversation was beginning to sound like a pity party for *moi*.

Erin was still babbling on. "I didn't mean to say that you're not—"

"It's okay, Erin," I interrupted. I had to stop her

from stumbling into another weird area. "And don't worry about the munchies. I'll swing by the store on the way to Kerri's."

After we hung up I sat at my desk and stared at the phone. *Do my friends really think of me that way?* I wondered. *Do my friends really think I'm that boring?*

Chapter 3

Kerri

"**L**et's clean this mess up before we get another rush," Frip said, tossing me a sponge. We were doing our usual Saturday evening shift at Bernie's Bagels, and I'd just finished making up a killer order for six sandwiches, all with different bagel types and condiments.

"I'll bet that's the last one," I said, checking the giant bagel clock on the wall. Almost seven. "Dinnertime is over." So was our shift, thank God. I was tired of standing, and I couldn't wait to tell my friends what Matt had said at the mall. Not that we always gave each other play-by-plays, but when something this good happens you've got to share the goods. "You on for next Saturday?" I asked Frip as I wiped some crumbs off the counter.

"Not supposed to be, but I could use the extra money," Frip said. "How about you?"

"I'll be gone. In Chicago for the senior trip."

"Cool," he called as he went off to check the coffee urns.

I nodded. Way cool. I would finally be able to put aside everything else and totally focus on my boyfriend. And the best part was that Matt was looking forward to the trip so that he could be with me too.

I rinsed the sponge and went out from behind the counter to wipe down tables. The door opened behind me, startling me. A girl with chin-length brown hair came in and went up to the counter. I'd never seen her before, but something about her reminded me of Donna.

Donna.

I remembered the day Donna had shown up at Bernie's. She'd seemed so innocent at first. Almost sweet.

But I'd misjudged her in a big way. She wasn't sweet or innocent. Not the girl who'd steered her Volkswagen Jetta toward me and hit the gas. I could still see the sick look on her face—almost a smile.

The sponge slipped out of my fingers as I closed my eyes, remembering the way the gravel flew under the wheels, the awful feeling in my stomach, the shriek of the tires. I began to shiver— not from cold, but from the same fear I'd felt that day. I straightened up and crossed my arms, trying to stop the trembling.

"Hey, Kerri . . ." Frip came over from the behind the counter and touched my shoulder. "You don't look so good. Do you feel okay?"

I shook my head. "Yeah," I lied. "But I'd like to cut out early, if it's okay. Think you can cover for me?"

"No problem," Frip said. "Our shift ends in fifteen minutes anyway. Go on, get a head start on your wild Saturday night."

"Thanks," I said, ducking into the back room for my coat. I wasn't shivering anymore, but I still felt this desperate need to get out of the place where Donna had tracked me down. I couldn't believe the way I'd fallen apart, just thinking about her. Was she going to haunt me forever?

As I stepped out of Bernie's, the wave of cold evening air reminded me it wouldn't be so easy to get home, since my car was in the shop. I trudged over to the bus stop, still thinking about Donna. I wanted to get past this thing. I really did. *Don't let her hurt you anymore,* I told myself. *It's up to you to quit thinking about her.*

At the bus stop I stood behind some college kids, breathing in and out carefully. It was one of my mother's meditation tricks . . . good air in, bad air out. Not that I really believed in that New Age stuff, but at the moment I was willing to try anything.

A car pulled into the bus stop, the passenger's window sliding down. "Kerri! I thought that was you," said a male voice.

Bending my knees, I leaned down to peer into the car from a distance. After my dark thoughts of Donna, I felt a little defensive. The guy behind the wheel was wearing a beat-up leather jacket and red scarf. Relief. It was a friendly, familiar face.

"Hey, Stewart," I said. He'd been in one of Jessica's classes at the U, and she'd introduced us when Stewart needed a model for his portfolio. From there, we'd become friends, and Stewart had helped me put together my head shots—a must if I wanted to be a real model. Which I did. It would definitely pay better than the minimum wage at Bernie's Bagels, and it would definitely help pay for my college tuition next year at the University of Miami.

"Need a ride somewhere?" he asked.

"Yeah!" I jumped into the car and buckled up. "I just got out of work, and my car's in the shop."

"Well, cars do break down," Stewart said, pulling away from the curb. "Where to?"

"Home. I'm having some friends over."

"And you didn't invite me?" Stewart pouted, acting insulted.

"Girlfriends," I said. "Sorry, dude, but you're the wrong gender."

"Maybe next time," he said, and for a moment I wondered if he was flirting with me. I decided to change the subject. Stay on the safe side.

"How's everything at the studio?" I asked. Stewart often worked as his uncle's photography assistant.

"Things arc cool." He ran his hand through his shaggy brown hair. "I'm just coming from there. Been doing a lot of grunt work, but it's an education just being around the shoots."

I felt a twinge of jealousy. Not that I wanted to be a photographer. But if all these shoots were going on at his uncle's studio, why hadn't I gotten work? I'd done a runway show at the mall. I'd even been approached by someone from a Milwaukee modeling agency.

"How about you?" Stewart asked, digging into my wounded ego. "Did anything ever happen with that agency? What was their name . . . Funny Face?"

"Ha, ha," I said, "but it's just Face." I looked out the window, trying to pretend I didn't care that I hadn't heard from the agency. "I sent them my headshot, but so far I haven't heard from them."

"Really?" Stewart seemed surprised. "With those awesome pictures I did for you?"

"They were pretty good," I admitted, half grinning. "Just not good enough, I guess. I'd love to do some real modeling. But I don't know what my next move should be."

"I just heard about something," Stewart said. He stepped on the brake pedal at a red light, then reached into the backseat. "Check this out." He handed me a piece of paper.

The letterhead was from the Diamond Agency, with a Chicago address. Across the top it said: PARENTAL CONSENT FORM.

"What's this?" I asked.

"A bunch of those were faxed to Uncle Bob's studio. Apparently they're looking for some new faces. They've got an open call for young models, so every girl who's under eighteen needs one of these forms."

"No way!" I picked up the paper. "This is awesome."

"Of course, you have to get your butt to Chicago sometime soon."

I held the paper to my chest and smiled. "This is perfect timing. I'll be there next week for a class trip."

"No kidding?" Stewart turned into the garden apartment complex where I lived with my mom and my older brother, Dan. "So do it, Kerri. Give Diamond a call."

My thoughts flashed to the runway show I'd done at the mall. I'd made so much money for just a few hours of work. Actually, a few hours of fun—except for Donna, of course. She'd popped up in the audience, trying to throw me off guard. But I'd finished the show just fine.

I took a deep breath, trying to shake Donna from my mind. I wanted to stop letting her ruin my life.

Chicago would be different. My chance for a new start with Matt and modeling. Running into Stewart was a stroke of luck tonight—sort of like kismet.

"Thanks a lot, Stewart," I said, smoothing out the permission form. "This is great." I told him where to pull up beside my building.

"Cool," he said, turning to smile at me. "I'm outta here. I'm actually helping a friend do a wedding gig tonight. But maybe we can catch a movie sometime."

I smiled at him, not wanting to hurt his feelings. "That'd be nice, but I don't think my boyfriend would appreciate it."

He squinted at me. "You still hanging around with that football player?"

I nodded. "What can I say? I'm a sucker for running backs."

"That's scary," Stewart teased, touching my shoulder. "Good luck in Chicago."

"Thanks," I said, thinking about the trip. My chance to get a real modeling job. My chance to get closer than ever with my boyfriend. I couldn't wait for Monday morning.

The Saturday night sleepover was in progress in my room.

Erin and Maya were stretched out on my bed, leafing through tour books of Chicago.

"Ooh, this is good. I need a pen to take notes." Erin jumped off the bed and straightened her oversized T-shirt. She grabbed a pen from my desk and jumped back onto the bed. "There are these grungy, hip neighborhoods of galleries and clubs and cafés where all the creative types hang out. Bucktown . . . and Wicker Park. We've got to check them out."

"Put them on the list," Maya said, pushing a clipboard with a list of "Must Sees" across my bed.

"Already on it," Erin answered, not looking up.

"Sometimes online research just doesn't

work." Jessica sat at the computer clicking on websites. She needed to get some ideas for her "Dear Jessica" column, which was supposed to start up after the trip. "I just can't find what I need. I must be using the wrong keywords."

"You need teen crises?" Erin asked. "I'd think that would be a no-brainer."

"Really," I said. "Give me a minute, I'll give you a teen problem. I'm being haunted by a teen stalker. My dad disappeared when I was ten. My brother won't grow up and get out of the apartment. I'm about half a million dollars short for college. All fantastic! All true!"

We laughed.

"Nah," Jessica said. "Your problems are too sensational to be believed. Except for Dan. That cling-on brother thing happens a lot."

I sat cross-legged on the floor, trying to locate the Diamond Agency on a map of Chicago.

"This book says the first thing you should do is see Chicago from one of the tall buildings," Maya said. "But I can't wait to hit the Magnificent Mile. It's a stretch of swanky stores."

"Hey, they've got a Hard Rock Café there," Erin said.

I only half listened as my finger followed the line of Smith Avenue, where the modeling agency was located. "This is right near the pier. It should be easy to find once we get to Chicago." Of course, I'd already spilled the whole story about how I'd run into Stewart and heard about the open call at the Diamond Agency. "Now I've just got to find time to get there."

"Don't forget about that permission form," Maya reminded me. "You need your mother's signature."

"That's right." I reached up and fumbled on my desk to find it so I could take another look at it. Even though it was just an ordinary faxed form, it seemed to contain magical possibilities. "I'll have Mom sign it as soon as she gets back."

There was a knock on the half-open door, and my brother, Dan, poked his head in. "I'm leaving," he said, pulling a watch cap over his stubbly blond hair. "I take it you girls can be trusted not to burn the place down or anything?" Dan is twenty-one and I'm seventeen, but he still acts as if I'm a pesky ten-year-old.

"We are definitely not to be trusted," Erin teased, one brow arching. "But we gave up playing with matches years ago."

"Hot date?" I asked.

Dan ignored the question. "Tell Mom I won't be too late," he said, turning away.

"Do you mean late in this time zone, or is that Dan time?" I called after him.

"Just tell her," he called back. Dan and I don't have the coziest relationship in the world, but we get along.

"What's Liz doing tonight?" Erin asked. "Yoga? Karate? Or having a Tarot reading?"

My mother is always trying out New Age things. Crystals, feng shui, astrology, candles, macrobiotics. "Good guess," I said. "But she's out with Yucky Chucky."

"Ew." Maya wrinkled her nose, knowing how I felt about my mom's boyfriend, Chuck Berman— that he was too young and too full of himself to be dating my mom. At least Maya and I had that in common—our parents were dating annoying people. "Why is it that the bad matches just seem to stick?" Maya asked.

"Please, don't curse me," I said. "Mom doesn't seem too serious about Chuck. I mean, how could she? He's only in grad school."

"Sounds like you need a break," Erin said. "We all do."

"Let's make a pact," Jessica said, spinning around in my computer chair to face us. "Let's have a blowout, incredibly awesome time on this trip."

"Agreed," Maya said.

"I'm in," Erin added.

"Me too." I glanced back at the permission form in my hand. We all had big expectations for this trip, and mine were increasing by the minute.

"Do you think Liz will sign that form?" Maya asked. "I mean, how does she feel about the modeling thing?"

"She's fine with it," I said.

"She's fine with everything," Erin said. "Liz is the coolest mother in the world. You are so lucky, Kerri. You can do just about anything you want."

I heard the front door open out in the hall. Yucky Chucky's low voice rumbled. Mom laughed. "We're in here!" I called. A moment later, Mom appeared in the doorway, with Chuck peering over her shoulder.

"Hey, girls," he said, raking one hand over his head back toward his ponytail. A greasy ponytail, as usual. Or was that mousse? Either way, I hoped Mom wasn't getting close enough to touch that thing. "What's the four-one-one?" Chuck asked.

Oh, stop trying to sound cool, I wanted to say. Jessica and Maya didn't seem to notice, but Erin flashed me a look that confirmed what I was thinking—*total freak*.

"Just hanging in my crib with the homies," I replied as seriously as I could.

Erin covered her mouth to keep from laughing out loud.

"We just caught the new Kate Winslet movie," Mom said. "Thumbs up!" she exclaimed so enthusiastically her shoulder-length blond hair bobbed. "I'm going to make some green tea."

"Oh, Mom," I called. The paper fluttered in my hand as I stood up. "Dan went out. And I need you to sign this."

She took the form, her forehead creasing as she read it. "What's this?"

"It just says that you give me permission to do this go-see in Chicago. I'll fit it into my schedule during the class trip, and it could be really cool. A friend of mine told me they're looking for new faces."

"New faces?" Chuck repeated, grinning. "As opposed to old faces? Is that a ridiculous expression or what?"

Inside, I groaned. Chuck's amateur philosophical semantics drove me nuts, but I usually managed to restrain myself and wait for him to leave. I stared at Mom, willing her to sign the form and save us from Chuck.

She bit her lower lip as she read over the form. Not her usual, jump-for-joy response. All the animation seemed to drain from her face.

"You just need to sign the bottom." I handed her a pen, but she didn't take it.

"I'm sorry, Kerri," Mom said, giving the form back to me. "But I'm not going to sign this."

Chapter 4

I stared at the form in her hand. "What do you mean, you're not going to sign it?"

My friends were silent. No one was used to seeing my mom say no.

Mom placed the form on my desk and touched my arm in that gentle mom way. "I really can't see you modeling on that level," she said. "It's one thing to take a job or two in Madison. But that world is so superficial. It's not you. And it was never in your plans, right? What about college? You've been talking for years about going into physical therapy."

I shrugged. "None of that's changed."

"But modeling in Chicago?" Mom shook her head. "That would change things. We're talking major commitment. It would suck up all your time and energy. Besides, it's against everything you believe in, Kerri."

"It's not a religion, Mom," I insisted. "It's

modeling, and I have no problem with dressing up and looking good."

Mom shook her head sadly. "You know that true beauty lies within . . . it's in a person's essence, in the spirit that transcends the physical shell."

"Too true," Chuck said, his ponytail bobbing as he nodded.

He was the last person I wanted to take advice from. Especially advice on spirituality. Ha! The guy had about as much character as the back of a cereal box. Last month I found out he listened to heavy metal music. Case closed.

I crossed my arms, feeling defensive. My mother was a good listener. I knew she'd respect my opinion if I stood firm. "Mom, this is such a great opportunity. I've got to go for it."

"No, honey. This is a definite no."

I swallowed, not sure what to say, not sure how to win here. Mom and I didn't usually argue. When your mom always says yes, why fight it?

"Wait one second," I told Mom, hands on my hips. "This is totally unfair. Can't you see how important this is to me?" My voice was getting louder, but I couldn't help it.

Mom sighed. "I've made my decision."

"Without thinking of me!" I shouted. "Mom, this is my ticket to Miami! We're talking big bucks here. Or would you rather see me getting carpal tunnel from buttering bagels and just making a few puny dollars for it?"

"It's a matter of ethics, not money," Mom said. She turned away. "That's it, Kerri. Discussion over."

"What?" I squeaked.

"Your mother is right, Kerri," Chuck chimed in. "This is really the best thing for you."

"As if that's any of your business," I told him. "Don't you have some *homework* to do?"

That shut him down. He turned and headed out to the living room. I slammed the bedroom door closed and collapsed against it, sinking down to the floor. "My mother has lost it. This is so unfair!" I moaned.

Maya gave me a hand up and sat me down on the bed between Erin and her.

"It stinks," Jessica agreed.

"Totally unfair," Erin said, twirling her dark hair into a bun and sticking a pencil in to keep it in place. "But try to have some perspective. So your mom doesn't want you to be a model. It's probably the first time she's ever said no to you. Not like my parents, who usually say no before they've even heard the question."

"Okay, you definitely have me beat on the crisis front," I admitted. "But that doesn't make me feel a whole lot better."

"We can wallow in our misery together," Erin said. "Wallow, wallow."

"You guys need a total distraction," Maya said. She turned to Jessica. "Did you bring the munchies?"

Jessica nodded. "Yeah, but they're out in the kitchen with Yucky Chucky."

"Oh, great," I said. "He's going to contaminate them."

Maya giggled. "Good thing we all had our cootie shots when we were seven."

We all laughed, and I was glad my friends were there to break the tension. "I do have a secret stash of pizza bagels in the freezer," I said. "But I offer them up only if you guys help me persuade Mom to sign this."

Jessica gave me a sharp look. "Not in this millennium."

"I don't know," Erin said. "Sounds like Liz is hanging tough. This might be one battle you have to surrender."

"No way," I insisted, not wanting to admit Erin might be right. Because deep down inside, I knew Mom wasn't going to sign this, and that hurt. I unrolled the permission slip and read it again. It was short. Just name, address, phone number, and signature. How could such a simple thing be such a huge obstacle?

I leaned over toward Jess again. "Pen, please?"

She handed me a black felt-tip pen. I put the form over the papers on Maya's clipboard and began to fill in the blanks.

"Kerri?" Jessica's voice had an edge in it. I smelled disapproval. "What are you doing?"

"Filling out this form," I answered without looking up.

"But your mom won't sign it," Jess said. "What's the point?"

My hand slid down to the signature line. I took a deep breath, then set the pen in motion. In my best imitation-Mom handwriting I wrote my mother's name. "There. I don't need Mom to sign it anymore."

A look of horror filled Jess's eyes as she saw what I'd done. "Kerri . . ." She lowered her voice. I guess she was afraid my mom would hear us. "You can't do this. What if your mom finds out you signed her name?"

Erin looked up from her guidebook and grinned. "A forgery? Aren't you the *crafty* girl."

Maya giggled, but Jessica didn't budge. "It's not funny. Come on, Kerri. You're not serious about this, are you?"

"Oh, Jess, please don't make me feel guilty." I handed the form to her. "Since you're already there, will you do the honors? I need to scan this into the computer, along with a headshot. I can e-mail it to the Diamond Agency now, and they'll have it on file when I call Monday morning."

Jessica took the form. "Are you sure?"

"Lighten up, Jess." I put my hands on her shoulders and gave her a gentle shake. "Don't you see? Sometimes the only way to get what you want is by breaking the rules."

Jessica

Monday dawned, gray and chilly and kind of disappointing. Teachers were checking off attendance and directing kids to line up for one of the buses. Dancing from one foot to another to stay warm, I watched my breath form white puffs in the air and waited my turn to board a bus. I'd managed to get all my work done, except the stuff for my column. I figured I could come up with some ideas during the trip.

Senior Trip. Whoopee! I thought, wishing I really felt that way. I knew I'd have a good time once we got to Chicago, but now, as I waited in line behind Kerri and Matt, a tiny obstacle occurred to me. The couples thing.

It was playing out before my eyes. Kerri cuddled up to Matt. Maya laughed over something Luke said. Erin jumped on Glen's back and insisted he carry her onto the bus.

In the back of my mind, I'd been thinking of the nonstop fun I'd have with my friends. I'd forgotten that they were ready to have fun with their boyfriends—a commodity that was scarce in my life at the moment.

I climbed the steps of the bus and followed Kerri down the aisle. In the middle of telling a story, she plunked into a seat beside Matt and continued talking. Behind her sat Luke and Maya, silent but snuggling. Across the aisle, Erin and Glen were adjusting their seats. *Very cozy*, I thought as I took the seat behind them. Alone.

And here I was about to embark on a job giving advice to other teenagers. Hard to believe. *I should probably write* myself *a letter*, I thought.

Dear Jessica,

All my friends have boyfriends, and it's driving me nuts. It simply underlines the fact that I am guyless. Help! Send boy. Tall, cute, smart and sincere.

Believe me, I knew a boyfriend couldn't solve all your problems. But the trip might be more fun with a guy to hang with.

"Everyone here?" called Mr. Calvert. He stood at the front of the bus, waving at some guys. "Let's take our seats so we can get going."

I wondered how we got lucky enough to have Mr. Calvert as our chaperone. He is our chorus teacher and the coolest adult in the school. I knew there were hard-nosed teachers on the other buses, but I figured Mr. Calvert would keep them relaxed.

The door slammed closed, the engine revved, and our bus rolled out of the parking lot.

Luke leaned close to Kerri's seat. "So, Kerri, Maya told me you might get a big-time modeling gig with an agency in Chicago."

"Actually, this is just a preliminary thing," Kerri pointed out. "First I need to get the agency to take me on. Then they'll send me out on go-sees, looking for work."

"In Chicago," I said, touching Kerri's arm across the aisle. "Don't you think your mom will be suspicious when you start spending so much time in another city?"

"That's all down the road," Kerri said. Her eyes sparkled as she spoke.

I could tell that she was thrilled, but this whole thing still seemed wrong to me. I knew Liz would flip when she found out about the forgery. If I did something like that my parents would ground me for the rest of senior year. Maybe into college, if they could. "Kerri . . ." I said quietly.

Kerri turned to me. "Looking out for me again, Jess? I'll be fine. Especially if I get a job."

"You will," Matt said, pulling her back in their seat. "Who wouldn't hire the most gorgeous girl in the world?"

Kerri disappeared from the aisle, but Maya leaned across and looked up front to make sure Mr. Calvert was in his seat. "Kerri," she called in a low voice. "When are you planning to go to the agency?"

"Whenever they can squeeze me in." Kerri's head popped back into the aisle. "I might have to ditch part of the class trip."

"We'll cover for you," Erin offered. "But you'll need a good story."

I stared down the aisle, wondering why I was the only one who had problems with this scenario.

"You could fake being sick," Matt suggested.

"Or tell them your father is in town and you're meeting him for lunch," Maya said. Kerri's parents got divorced seven years ago, and her dad kind of disappeared. This year, Kerri tracked him down in Milwaukee, and since then they've sort of kept in touch.

"No, *I've* got it!" Erin said. "You were trapped

in an elevator . . . at Marshall Fields or something. And the only thing that got you through it was the Snickers bar you always keep in your backpack."

"The Snickers story," Kerri said with a laugh. "That's a good one."

"Hel-lo?" I couldn't let this go on. "Guys, do you hear yourselves? This can't be a good thing if you've got to *concoct* a bunch of lame lies." The moment the words flew out I clamped my mouth shut. Did I really say that? Did I really use the word concoct? Maybe my friends had a point about the nerd factor creeping up on me.

"I thought the Snickers in the elevator was creative," Erin teased me. "Come on, Jess. Back off the good-girl routine for once."

"Really," Matt said. "This is Kerri's big chance."

"I . . ." But what could I say? "I just don't want Kerri to get in trouble," I finished.

"Jess is just trying to protect me," Kerri told everyone. "Besides, she can't help herself. Bending the rules just isn't her thing."

I opened my mouth to argue, but the words didn't come out. Because Kerri was right. I don't break rules. I do my best to follow instructions, make deadlines, ace tests, turn in perfect papers. I always try to do the right thing. But suddenly that sounded so geeky.

My friends went on making up ways for Kerri to ditch the teachers, but I just sat back in my seat and stared out the window as we passed a blue lake.

So this was Senior Trip. A real adventure. A time to bond with my best friends—me, myself, and I. Thinking of my column, I rewrote the last letter in my head:

Dear Jessica,

It's the strangest thing. I'm surrounded by friends, but sometimes I feel so alone. . . .

Chapter 5

Kerri

"**O**kay, people, listen up!" Mr. Calvert held up his hands in the crowded lobby, where Matt and I sat on our overstuffed duffel bags. Around me, students and piles of luggage were everywhere. We'd taken over the place already. At the check-in desk, phones were buzzing and guests were lined up, waiting to get their room keys. The whole scene was wonderfully insane, and I loved it.

"There are a few ground rules," called Ms. Gomes, my calculus teacher. She had a deep, raspy voice, bold black glasses, and flawless brown skin. "Follow the rules, and you'll have no problem. Break the rules, and you'll find yourself on a bus headed home."

"Eek," I said, pretending to hide behind Matt. My hands slipped over his arms and I leaned my face against his shoulder. He reached back and held on to my waist, holding me close.

"As you know, there will be mandatory class tours each day," Ms. Gomes went on. "Don't make us come looking for you. . . . It won't be a pretty sight."

I leaned closer to Matt, feeling safe with him. He would be my protection against big, bad Ms. Gomes and her stern words. I'd heard that the teachers were pretty lax on Senior Trip, and I figured I could sneak away for a few hours if I had to. The Diamond Agency was definitely worth it.

"You will also have free time to explore the city," Ms. Gomes went on, "but we ask that you don't go anywhere alone. Stay with a friend or roommate. Your nighttime curfew is eleven thirty. And be forewarned, we *will* be checking rooms."

"We will find you," Matt whispered in my ear, imitating her. He leaned close, pressing his lips against the tender spot on my neck. "We *will* find you . . . and kiss you."

"Stop!" I giggled, not meaning it at all. I was thrilled that the trip was already off to a great start.

"Mrs. Chapp and I have your keys," Ms. Gomes went on. "You know your roommates by now. And we've put girls and boys on separate floors. Let it stay that way."

That brought a laugh.

Ms. Gomes looked up, adjusting her glasses.

"You can line up for your keys and take your luggage upstairs. We'll meet down here for the bus ride to the Art Institute in thirty minutes."

Everyone around us started moving at once. Matt stood and put out his hand. "Guess we should head up and check it out."

I grabbed his hand, and he pulled me up as Maya called out from across the lobby, "I'll get our keys!" We had decided to room together. Jessica and Erin were also sharing a room. I nodded at Maya and hoisted up my duffel bag.

"Want me to get that for you?" Matt offered.

"That's okay. I have to fend for myself," I told him, adjusting the strap. "Besides, we're on separate floors."

"Just an elevator ride away," Erin pointed out as she and Glen pushed past us.

We waited by the elevators, along with a big crowd of students, then packed ourselves in. A bunch of girls got out on the eighth floor, then our guys peeled off on the tenth.

Luke's hat fell to the floor, and Matt picked it up and waved him back. "Go for a pass. Go long, longer!" he shouted as Luke dropped his bags and dashed down the hall.

"It's been nice knowing you," Glen said, waving as the elevator doors started to close.

"Don't get excited, Daley," Erin called after him. "I've got your room number."

Alone with my friends in the elevator, I let out a shriek. "This is so great!" I waved my room key in the air. "We definitely need to figure out something with the guys. Some kind of code we can use in case one of us wants to be alone in the room with our boyfriend."

"It's called a Do Not Disturb sign," Erin said.

"I don't know about that," Maya said, biting her bottom lip. "Seems a little obvious. Ms. Gomes might be suspicious."

"True," Erin agreed. "But we definitely need a code if we're going to have the boys over."

The door opened, and we stepped out.

"Twelfth floor," Jessica announced. "Lingerie, sleepwear, and boyland amusement park."

We all laughed. "You're so creative," I told Jess. "You think of a code."

Jessica scrunched up her face. "I'm sorry, but I can't wrap my brain around that one. Probably because the possibility of me needing privacy with a guy anytime in the near future is a big zero."

"Come on, Jess, don't count yourself out," Maya said.

"Sorry, Jess." I put my hand on her arm, realizing that she was a little sensitive about the guy thing. Why hadn't that occurred to me before? We were all paired off, and Jess was here alone. That would bother anybody.

"It's okay," Jessica said. "Do I need a guy to have fun? No. I am an independent girl, responsible for her own emotional well-being." She tilted her head and smiled. "I've got to write that down, and use it for my column. Oops, I almost passed our room." She stuck her plastic key into the slot of room 1233, and the door clicked open.

I watched her go inside, relieved that she didn't seem to be too hurt. Once everything got started, I knew, Jessica would have fun. She always does.

"See you guys downstairs in a few," Erin said, following Jessica inside.

"Okay," I called. I wanted to wash up and call the Diamond Agency before I took another step.

"We're down here," Maya called to me.

Room 1238 was a few doors down on the opposite side of the hall. I dropped my bag onto a bed and opened the curtains to see the side of another building. "Great view of the brick wall next door," I told Maya.

With floral curtains, floral pictures, and a television bolted to its stand, the room was clean, but hardly deluxe. I splashed warm water on my face, and buried it in a towel.

"It's a little run-down, but it's ours," Maya said, lying back on a bed. "I think I'm going to like it here. This bed is comfy."

"Don't get too comfortable," I said, fixing my hair in the mirror. "We have to be downstairs for the trip to the Art Institute."

There was a knock on the door. "Who's there?" I called.

"Pizza delivery."

I swung the door open, and Luke nearly fell in. Matt was right behind him.

"Come on in!" I cried. They came into the room, and Matt sat on the dresser by the window.

"Hey, your room is bigger than mine," Luke said. "Mine is all bed." He bounced on the mattress next to Maya. "Nice."

"Got room for me?" Matt asked Luke. "I got paired up with Lloyd Thomas."

"Lloyd Thomas!" Maya and Luke and I said in unison. He was only the most antisocial senior in school. The guy actually pulled a desk to the back of the classroom to be away from the rest of us.

"How'd you get so lucky?" Maya teased Matt.

Matt shook his head. "That's what I get for forgetting to sign up for a roommate, I guess. But don't be surprised if you see me sleeping on the lobby couch downstairs. The guy said he's gonna sleep in the bathtub in protest, because he didn't want to room with anybody. That's so weird."

"Hey, quit rocking the boat," Maya said to Luke, who was still bouncing on the bed. But then she sat up and bounced beside him.

Matt turned away from a beam of sunshine sneaking in through the window. The way the light hit his brown hair, making it shimmer . . . mmm. I could have melted right there. "This is a great room. We should meet here for breakfast." He looked over at me. "Just us."

My heart pounded in my chest. The idea of being alone with him in this room was so romantic.

Unfortunately, Maya thought the "us" included her and Luke. "That'd be great. The Breakfast Club. We can smuggle up some food from the buffet downstairs."

"Cool." Luke stopped bouncing and pulled Maya down onto the bed. "Anything to break away from the pack. Traveling with every other senior from South Central High makes me feel like a herded animal."

"Poor Luke," Maya said.

"Don't tease me," he answered, tickling her ribs.

"Stop!" she squealed.

"We'd better get downstairs," I said, glancing at

the digital clock on the television. We had ten minutes. But first I really needed to call the Diamond Agency. I picked up the phone and read the instructions on how to dial out of the hotel.

"Who are you calling?" Maya asked through a giggle.

"The modeling agency. I need to see if I can get an appointment."

I dialed the number, as Maya kept giggling. "Shh!" I said, covering the mouthpiece as the line at the agency started ringing.

"Diamond Modeling Agency," a female voice answered.

"Hi. I'm Kerri Hopkins," I said, hoping she wouldn't hear Maya and Luke laughing in the background. "I heard you're having an open call for models, and I'm calling to see if I can make an appointment. I e-mailed my headshot and a permission form."

"Please hold." After a moment she came back and told me the agency could see me tomorrow. "Open call is first thing in the morning. Nine o'clock. You don't need an appointment."

"I guess I could be there by nine," I said.

Across the room, Matt winced and mouthed, A.M.? I nodded, and he collapsed on my bed. I managed to control my laughter—at least until after I'd hung up.

"I'm sorry!" I said. "But I had to jump on it. It's not like I can be picky."

Luke was still tickling Maya on the bed. "Oh, Kerri, you'll . . . miss . . . the . . . Breakfast . . . Club," she said between giggles.

I went over to the foot of my bed. "I'm really sorry, Matt."

"Don't be." He lifted his head, then stood up in front of me. "We'll miss you, but I understand."

"You do?" I asked. That was when he pulled me close, sending a wave of sensation through me. I was so relieved that he understood. I leaned against him, soaking up his warmth. He kissed me, and I wrapped my arms around his broad shoulders. Oh, it felt so good to be here with him.

The kiss ended, but he still held me close. "This is your big chance, Kerri," he whispered in my ear. "Go for it."

Jessica

"This is one place I've always wanted to visit," Erin said as we crossed the wide sidewalk in front of the Art Institute of Chicago.

"Me too," I said. When I studied art history in tenth grade, Ms. Vittliano had raved about the works of art at the Institute. My favorite paintings were those done by the Impressionists, and there was a whole section devoted to that period here.

Ahead of us, Matt and Kerri were already posing beside one of the two lion statues that sat at the main entrance, while Maya snapped a photo. Matt reached up and patted the lion's mane, telling him, "Hey, it's a jungle out there."

"Lame!" Kerri said, pinging Matt's shoulder. Then they both laughed.

Beside me, Glen sneaked up on Erin and slid his arms around her waist. "Ooh!" she gasped, swinging around in his arms. "You scared me."

I looked down at the assignment in my hand, wishing I could disappear into the crowd. All this happy couple stuff was kind of getting to me. *Stop it, Jess,* I told myself. *These are your friends. You can hang out with them without being part of a couple too.*

Matt pulled Kerri against a marble wall and pinned her there for a kiss. I glanced away, only to see Luke take Maya's hand. I squeezed my eyes closed, trying not to feel uncomfortable with all this kissy stuff. But it wasn't working.

"So which painting are we going to see?" Maya asked, pressing against my shoulder to read the handout from the teachers.

"Here are our choices," I said, reading from the paper. "Edward Hopper's *Nighthawks*. Pablo Picasso's *The Old Guitarist*. Or Georges Seurat's *A Sunday on La Grande Jatte—1884.*"

"Picasso," Luke said. "I wrote a paper on him once. Maybe some of it will come back to me."

"Sounds good," Matt said, checking his watch. "Pablo's the man."

"Pab-lo, Pab-lo," Luke started chanting.

Glen and Matt and Kerri joined in, as if they were rooting for a player in a football game. From what I'd read about Picasso, the cheer would have fed his enormous ego. It wasn't the painting I wanted to see.

"Anybody want to see the Seurat?" I asked. "I mean, there's a musical written about it, *Sunday in the Park with George*. And I've always wanted to see that anyway."

"I might head over there after the Picasso," Erin said.

But she was the only one who answered. The group seemed to have a life of its own, and it was headed toward the Picasso painting. Everyone but Erin was ahead of me, pushing through the doors to the cavernous marbled room and handing in their admissions passes at the entrance.

At first I felt left behind, but then I realized this

was the perfect opportunity. I could wander off alone, soak up some incredible art, and give my friends some privacy with their boyfriends. "You know what?" I said to Erin. "I'm going to split off and find the Seurat. How about if I meet you guys in the museum caf?"

Erin paused, her dark eyes touched with concern. "Are you sure? I can go with you if you want."

I knew she was feeling sorry for me, trying to be nice, but I was sort of relieved at the idea of exploring on my own. "No, I'm okay. Actually, I'd sort of like to go it alone for a while. Catch you in about an hour, okay?"

We both picked up maps from the information desk, and Erin hurried off to catch up with the others. "See you later, Jess."

I made my way through a skylighted central court full of sculptures. Then I found my way to the Impressionist collection.

Weaving through rooms filled with beautiful oil paintings in pastel colors, I finally spotted Seurat's painting. A handful of people stood in front of it, and as they moved away I noticed a familiar person sitting on a nearby bench.

Alex. My old boyfriend.

I stopped in my tracks. The last people I

wanted to see were Alex and his new girlfriend, Suzanne. After two years of being in love and breaking his heart, then letting him break mine, I had gone through some difficult times with Alex. But I'd finally gotten over him. I moved on. Alex didn't. For some reason, he wouldn't give me the time of day.

Okay, maybe the reason was that I'd cheated on Alex with Scott, that college guy. Guilty. I knew it was wrong, but I'd done everything I could think of to make it up to him.

I glanced at the painting in the distance, then back at Alex. Where was Suzanne? Nowhere to be seen. Though Alex was the real obstacle. *Maybe I should go to another painting,* I thought. *Why didn't I just settle for the Picasso?* I started to back away, then paused. Why should I have to change my plans just because Alex had a problem? I was going to be adult about this. Maybe he wouldn't even notice I was there.

Gritting my teeth, I walked up behind him and sat on the far end of his bench to study the painting. The greens and blues looked so crisp and refreshing, and for a moment I wished I could be transported into the landscape of the people picnicking near the water around the turn of the century. Women with parasols, dogs, children . . .

There was a flurry of movement beside me. A sideways glance told me Alex was looking at me, but when I turned my head, he quickly turned away. *Cold shoulder*, I thought. *Nothing new about that.*

I wasn't staring at him, but I could feel him stand up. I assumed he was going to leave, but instead he came closer and sat right next to me on the bench. "Cool painting," he said.

"Yeah." I couldn't believe he'd spoken to me. Feeling gutsy, I decided to go a little further. "Where's Suzanne?" I asked.

"Not here. Her mother wouldn't let her come on the trip."

"Really?" I was surprised. I'd just assumed that she'd been on the other bus with Alex, snuggling the whole way here.

"Suzanne's mother has a problem with overnight class trips," Alex said. "I don't know why."

"Hmm." I could just imagine. "Girls and guys alone in a hotel? Staying out all night? Wandering the streets of a strange city?" I shrugged. "I don't know why she'd object to that."

Alex laughed, and I found myself smiling. The tension was broken, and for a second we connected, sort of like old times. No. Not like old times. Kind of like . . . friends.

Then Alex closed his notebook, and the moment faded.

Gone.

"See ya," he said, heading off.

Two other people sat in his spot immediately, and the universe seemed to expand around me. I was back to being Jessica the girl without a parasol, sitting alone and staring at a painting of happy people in a beautiful park on a summer day.

I flipped open my notebook and wrote:

Dear Jessica,

Field. Trips. Suck.

Chapter 6

Kerri

"**M**y ears are popping!" I said, squeezing Matt's hand as the Skydeck elevator shot up. We were riding up to the 103rd story of the Sears Tower for our last class assignment of the day.

"That's nothing," Matt said. "I left my stomach somewhere around the fortieth floor."

"Could be a problem," I said, resting my head on his shoulder for a minute. My friends and I were stuffed into the elevator, along with a dozen or so other tourists. Erin and Glen held hands over by the doors, and Luke had his arm around Maya. Jessica stood beside them, her hands stuffed in the pockets of her jacket, and I wondered if she still felt out of place.

"Did I ever tell you I have a fear of heights?" Glen told Erin. "I get queasy whenever I go up the stairs to school."

"That's because Mr. Montefiore's toupee wigs

you out," Erin responded. "He's on the third floor."

We all laughed.

"Trapped in an elevator with the odd couple," Jessica said. Turning to the elevator operator, she asked, "Does this thing go any faster?"

More laughs. And from Jess's smile I could see she was enjoying the moment. I straightened up and grinned at her, glad that she was having a better time.

The elevator slowed, then the operator opened the doors. We stepped out into a bright room with floor-to-ceiling windows.

"Awesome," Matt said as we took in the vista around us. The sky had cleared, with only a few high clouds dotting the horizon.

"We need to find a guide," Erin said. "I hear that on a clear day, you can see Michigan, Indiana, and even Wisconsin."

I moved forward, toward the windowed wall. The city of Chicago looked so orderly below, with a neat grid of streets and twisting canals leading to the expansive, sparkling blue of Lake Michigan. Beyond the city, land stretched out, flat and green, for miles.

"It really is an awesome view," I said, feeling my toes tingle as we stepped up to the glass. Seeing the city and lake and land stretched out before me,

I felt empowered. The world was at my fingertips. I was going for an interview at a Chicago modeling agency tomorrow. I was off in a big city with my best friends and the guy I loved.

Anything could happen. A million wonderful things could easily happen here in Chicago.

Erin and Glen waved us over to the other side of the deck. "Hey, check it out," Erin said. "You can see Wisconsin from here."

We joined them, comparing the landscape to the map on the sign beside the window.

"I see it," Matt said, squinting. "Actually, I see Madison. Yeah, there's your mother, Daley. She's taking out the trash."

"Really?" Glen pretended to stare off in the distance. "No, Matt, I think that's your mom. She's walking the dog. No—oops, that's your father."

We all laughed.

"There's the Shedd Aquarium," Maya pointed out. "It's on tomorrow morning's agenda."

"Looks like I'm going to be sick for that one," I said, smiling.

Matt nodded. "Me too. While you're off at the agency, I'm going to head over to the box office and see if we can score some Gaylord tickets."

"I thought you were getting them online," I said.

He shook his head. "They were sold out, but there are still some tickets available at the box office."

I didn't care much about Duke Gaylord, but I knew how important the concert was to Matt. "You'd do that for me?" I asked.

His blue eyes shimmered as he slid his arms around my waist. "Absolutely."

"You know, we are going to have a great time at that concert," I said, suddenly glad that none of my friends had been interested. "Just the two of us, hanging out."

Matt smiled and pulled me close for a kiss.

I closed my eyes, realizing how good it felt to be in his arms. How this trip was really going to seal our relationship. Forever. For always.

Jessica

Truth or Dare. I'd never liked the game much until tonight. We were hanging out in my room, and the game was well under way. Erin and Maya had already completed their dares. Kerri had disappeared not so mysteriously with Matt.

"Okay, okay," Luke said, rubbing his hands together. "Who's in the hot seat next?" He pressed his face to Maya's ear, adding, "How about you?"

"No way," Maya said, smiling. "I already did my dare, with the souvenir to prove it." She held up the umbrella she'd gotten out of the hotel's lost and found at the front desk. "Pick on somebody else," she said, "and dare them to put this back!"

I pulled my feet closer, hoping no one would notice me. From my perch, sitting cross-legged on the dresser, I realized I was enjoying this game as long as I didn't have to do the dare myself.

Especially tonight. Since we were in a mixed crowd, most of the dares had been kind of racy. Hannah Doyko had already kissed Tim Gardner (even though she was dating Jon Applebaum), and uptight Amber Brawley had licked Turtle Donovan's ear. Wonders never ceased.

At least I wasn't completely alone in this. Maya and Erin were here for moral support, but they were more adventurous. They also had their boyfriends to lean on. I crossed my fingers, hoping they wouldn't dare me to lick Turtle's other ear.

"How about Turtle?" Glen proposed.

"Come on, man!" Turtle sat back against the headboard, his heavy bulk shaking the bed. I was sure that weight came in handy for playing football, but it made him seem older than his seventeen years. "I already got my ear licked. That doesn't count?"

"It was Amber's dare," Erin pointed out.

Turtle swiped back his hair and nodded. "Okay, okay, bring it on. I choose Dare. What do you dare me to do?"

Glen cocked one eyebrow as he went over to the door and pulled it open. "I dare you to run up and down the hall with your pants down."

Amber and her friends snickered.

Turtle jumped to his feet with a growl. "Okay, girls," he said. "Get ready for a real treat."

Maya covered her eyes dramatically. "Oh, Glen, I wish you hadn't said that."

We all watched as Turtle lumbered to the door and dropped his pants. They pooled around his ankles, revealing camouflage-pattern boxer shorts and hairy legs. I thought Amber's eyeballs were going to pop out.

Kids screamed, cheering him on. A few of us jumped down and went to the door to watch him parade up the hall. Since Turtle had left his pants dangling around his ankles, it wasn't the most graceful run. Passing two women waiting for the elevator, he said, "Excuse me, ladies," and tramped on. The women frowned, looking annoyed.

"Don't mind him," I called to them as the door opened and they stepped in. "We can't take him anywhere."

A group of men stepped out of the elevator, laughing as the doors closed.

"Is it over?" Maya called, still hiding her eyes.

Turtle had reached the far wall and was heading back. "Almost," I said. "Let's hope he's faster than hotel security."

Turtle galloped back, cut into the room, and dived onto the bed with a final growl. Everyone clapped and cheered.

"That's going to be a hard one to top," Glen said. "But whose turn is it next?" He looked around, then squinted at me. I turned away and stared at a spot on the carpet, hoping he'd move on. No such luck. "Next victim, Jessica Carvelli. Truth or Dare?"

My face felt hot as I pushed up and sat on the dresser again. "I'm not letting *anyone* see my underwear."

"Big surprise," Erin said. "She's going to pick Truth." She turned to Amber's group. "Jessica always picks Truth. She's not the daring type."

Thanks a lot, Erin, I thought.

"No kidding," said one of Amber's friends.

I blinked. The comment came from a guy I barely knew. I crossed my arms, a little surprised. Did *everyone* think I was boring? I was getting a little tired of hearing how I needed to loosen up, be more fun, and ignore my schoolwork. If people thought I was a geek, they really didn't know me. I loved having fun. Fun was my middle name. Really.

Lifting my chin, I shot Erin a willful look and answered, "I pick Dare."

Chapter 7

Turtle rolled over on the bed and scratched his head. "You know, I've got an idea." He sat up and shot me a mischievous grin. "I dare you to throw a big after-curfew party. Tomorrow night. Right here in your room."

My throat felt tight. Break curfew? I could get suspended!

I was about to tell them no way, but before the words could fly out of my mouth, I paused. What would they say if I backed out? I could hear them already. *Oh, we knew it! Big surprise. Boring Jessica doesn't take chances. She probably has homework and knitting to catch up on.*

Erin threw her arms into the air. "That is the best idea you've ever had, Turtle!"

Turtle grinned again. "Yeah, I thought it was solid."

"An after-curfew party," Erin went on. "I am so

psyched." She turned to me and smiled—a not-so-subtle nudge.

"Okay," I said, a little awed by my own decision. "I'm in. The party's in my room tomorrow night, and you're all invited."

Everyone cheered and whistled.

And I smiled to cover the fact that my insides were suddenly quivering. *Oh, God. What did I just say?*

Kerri

My heart pounded as Matt pressed his lips against mine for a magical, moving, very private kiss. At last, we were alone in my room, away from friends and teachers and football players and tourists, and the spark between us was stronger than ever.

We were sitting on the bed, but I pulled him back onto the mattress. "Are you sure Maya won't come in?" he asked.

"Absolutely not. I used the code."

"What's that?"

"The Do Not Disturb sign."

"That's a clever one." He lifted his head and tucked a pillow under his neck.

I rested my head against Matt's chest, glad to

be alone with him. He ran his hand up and down my arms, creating a tingling sensation that drove me wild. But Matt knew that.

"This is great," he said. "We never get a chance to be alone like this, and this room has the distinct advantage of being Lloyd-free." He paused. "There's no pillow in your bathtub, right?"

I smiled. "I certainly hope not." Matt's roommate sounded like a kook.

"I wish I could stay here tonight," Matt said. "Would you mind? At least here, I could get some sleep. . . ." He ran his hand down over my cheek to my neck, then kissed me lightly on the lips. "Or not. I could stay here and get no sleep."

My breath caught in my throat. I'd been thinking the same thing, but I wasn't completely sure about it. Besides, tonight was the worst possible night for me to lose sleep. "I like your idea," I said, "but I can't be tired when I walk into that modeling agency tomorrow."

"Yeah, I guess."

I could hear the disappointment in his voice. "Sorry," I said, reaching up to touch his hair. "We'll do it another night."

He didn't answer. Was he upset? Or was he just mellowing out? I didn't want him to think that the modeling was more important than our relationship together.

"Sorry about tomorrow," I added. "But it'll be the last commitment I have on this trip. Nothing will stop me from getting to that jazz concert. I hope you can get tickets."

"Me too. I'm going to head out first thing in the morning."

There was a knock on the door. "Probably Maya," I said, jumping off the rumpled bed to answer it. I swung the door open to find Ms. Gomes. She peered in the room while I fumbled to smooth back my hair. I knew she'd threatened to check rooms, but I didn't think she'd actually *do* it.

"Curfew patrol," she said. Behind her, Maya danced up the hall, motioning to me helplessly. Ms. Gomes came into the room and stepped right up to the bed to stare at Matt. "Well, hello there. You don't look like the right gender to be this young lady's roommate."

"I'm here," Maya said, scurrying in the door.

"I'm just visiting," Matt said, standing up. He towered over the teacher, but her authority was unquestionable. "You know how you told us to stick close to a friend? Well, we took your advice."

"So I see," Ms. Gomes said, pointing Matt toward the door. "Glad that you can follow instructions. Here's my next command: Off to your room. Your *own* room."

"Got it," Matt said. He squeezed my hand as he passed by, then disappeared out the door.

"Good night," I called.

"Sleep tight," Ms. Gomes said, then pulled the door shut.

"Sorry," Maya said, pulling out her ponytail holder and brushing her hair. "By the time I saw her coming, it was too late."

"That's okay," I said. "We were just about to say good night, anyway. I've got to get my beauty sleep for tomorrow—if that's possible. I'm totally wired."

"Are you nervous about it?" Maya asked as she grabbed a tube of face scrub from her travel bag.

"Nervous. Excited. Thrilled. Worried. This is really important to me."

"You'll be great," Maya called from the bathroom over the sound of running water. "You always are. And guess what Jess is doing tomorrow?"

As we washed up and put on our nightshirts, she told me about the outrageous Truth or Dare game in which Jessica had agreed to throw a party.

"*Our* Jess?" I said, surprised. "Well, I guess she really is having a good time."

I was already in bed when Maya turned off the lights.

"So you're going to head out of here early," Maya said, "and I'm going to tell the teachers that you weren't feeling well and went back to bed."

"Right," I said. "Only you need to wait until you get to the aquarium. That way no one can run up to check on me. They wouldn't be too happy to find an empty bed. And don't tell Ms. Gomes—try Mr. Calvert."

"Got it. And if they call and there's no answer, you can just say you were too sick to come to the phone."

"Or that I was in the shower or something. I'm planning to meet you guys as soon as the interview is over, so I guess I'm in for a quick recovery."

"I wish I could go with you," Maya said.

"I'll be fine," I insisted, yawning. I decided to think about the dream I wanted to have before I fell asleep—maybe a glamorous party that Matt throws me after I grace the cover of my first magazine.

Yes . . . that would be perfect. . . .

We were on a boat. A beautiful ship, decorated with banners and flowers. I looked down at my dress, and it was straight out of a bridal magazine. A beautiful, flowing white gown, with lots of lace and beads and sheer chiffon. Oh, my God, I could barely hold back the tears of joy.

Matt and I were getting married! This was our wedding cruise.

And there were photographers everywhere, snapping pictures of me. I moved gracefully, shifting my magnolia bouquet, lifting my chin. They were pursuing me because I was a top model. The media was covering my wedding!

I turned to see Matt, so tall and handsome in his black tuxedo. As he took my hand, a light glinted in his blue eyes . . . that glimmer that told me he loved me. Forever. Tears welled in my eyes again. This time, they streamed down my cheeks to the deck of the boat.

So many tears. My feet were getting wet.

Very wet. Wait! The photographers were gone. Everyone was gone now—except for Matt. I glanced down and saw that water was gushing into the boat. It was already up to my knees.

"Matt!" I shrieked. "Our boat is sinking! What are we going to do?"

"It's okay," he said. "Don't you know how to swim?" He let go of my hand, went to the edge of the boat, and leaped into a huge swell of water.

Panicked, I spun around, trying to take a step in my soaked gown, but the water weighed me down. I couldn't swim. I couldn't do anything.

I spotted someone on the upper deck and cried

for help. Then I saw her face.

Donna. She stood there, smiling. Just smiling, as a swell of water rose up and choked me. . . .

I bolted up in bed with a gasp.

My nightshirt was soaked with sweat, and I was shaking. I glanced at the clock—almost six A.M. I didn't need to get up yet, but I couldn't go back to sleep. I couldn't go back to that boat.

Trembling, I slid my legs out of bed. I crossed the room, and turned on the bathroom light. My reflection in the mirror looked pale. My long blond hair seemed dull, and dark circles sat under my eyes. I hadn't slept well at all, haunted by that strange dream.

A wave of fear ran through my body as I thought of Donna. How she stared as the water swirled around me. How she stared and smiled as I died.

I rested my elbows on the vanity. Tears stung my eyes and dripped down my cheeks. *She's hundreds of miles away!* I scolded myself. *Why can't you get her out of your mind?*

Chapter 8

What am I doing here? I wondered as I looked around the posh waiting room of the Diamond Agency. With carpeting in a deep shade of mauve, large silk fans on the walls and gilded furniture upholstered in pink patterns, the room looked like a princess's court. So why did I feel like Cinderella waiting for her fairy godmother's magic wand? Maybe because I was so tired. Maybe because I was haunted by a dream that still made me shake to think about it.

Maybe because I was surrounded by beautiful girls. Girls with huge smiles. Girls with wholesome skin and dimples. Girls with long legs and even longer hair. Gorgeous girls who seemed very relaxed compared to me with my early morning jitters.

I tried to flip through a magazine, but a photo of a bride brought me right back to that scene on the boat. Everything had been so perfect—until we began to sink. And then Matt had acted so strange, so cold. He'd left me there.

I felt a lump rising in my throat, and I sat back and took a deep breath. I had to erase the nightmare from my mind and pull myself together for this interview. *I can, I will, I must. . . .*

A woman with skinny reading glasses and long, braided hair came out from the back and stopped at the reception desk. The other models in the waiting area got quiet and smiled up at her. We all knew she was golden—she worked here.

"Kerri Hopkins?" she called.

My heart raced as I jumped up, probably appearing way too eager. "That's me." Did I sound too perky? Or maybe too dull. I felt like I was losing my perspective, but I tried to focus as I followed her into a room of cubicles. *You can do this, Kerri,* I told myself.

"My name is Heidi. Have a seat," she said, pointing to a chair in her cube. "We've got to go over a few things before we get started. Let's see." She leafed through a file on her desk. "You're under age. That means—"

"But my mother signed the permission form," I interrupted, feeling a flash of paranoia.

"She did?" Heidi paged through the folder,

then clicked her tongue. "There it is. Okay, Karen."

"That's Kerri," I said, forcing a smile.

"Right . . ." Heidi squinted at me, then reached across her desk for a camera. "We need a shot for our files. Look at the camera, please." Before I had a chance to wet my lips or push back my hair, she snapped a shot, and the photo slid out the bottom. I blinked from the flash. Heidi left the camera and photo on the desk, then went back to my folder. "Okay, we've got your head shot, and it looks like you've filled everything out. Just sit tight."

She disappeared, leaving me to stare at a calendar with two panda bears on it and a bright red apple on her desk, which reminded me that I'd missed breakfast. Maya had a Power Bar in the room, but I'd been too shaken up by the dream to eat anything. The thought of drowning on my wedding day. And Donna's eerie smile. She had enjoyed every second of it. I wanted to cry, it seemed so pathetically sad, but again, I had to pull myself together. *Hel-lo! You're sitting at a modeling interview. Why don't you just burst into tears and ruin your chances?*

I waited there for at least ten minutes, starting to wonder if the teachers knew I was missing. What if Mr. Calvert panicked and called my mom? No, he wouldn't panic. I glanced at the phone on the desk, wondering if I should call Maya's cell to check in. But wait . . . they probably weren't even on the bus to the Shedd Aquarium yet.

Heidi returned with a measuring tape. "I need you to stand up," she said. "We have to get your measurements for the files."

I stood up, and she wrapped the tape around my bust, waist, and hips. Then she disappeared again.

More waiting. And I'd thought the dentist's office was bad.

At last, Heidi returned, this time munching on a cookie. She wiped the crumbs on her skirt as she told me, "They want to see you now."

"Who are they?" I asked, following her around the corner of her cube.

"The reps. Before we take on a model, all the reps need to see her in person."

"Okay," I said, really feeling like an amateur. I didn't know how these things were supposed to go. I expected a runway or a conference room, but Heidi just led me to a hallway, where she paused and knocked on a few doors.

"I have Karen here," she called out.

Two men and three women appeared, poking their heads out or leaning against the doorjamb.

"Actually, my name's Kerri," I told them. "And

I am from the land of cheese," I said, beaming a huge smile but trying not to gush.

Silence.

I felt a blush creep up my face. "You know . . . Wisconsin? We make, um . . . *cheese?*"

One of the reps rolled her eyes. And none of them spoke to me, they just stared. *Oh, boy,* I thought.

"Walk up and down the hall, Kerri," Heidi instructed.

I did, moving slowly and trying to exude confidence, but I couldn't help wishing that I'd rethought the stupid joke.

"Okay." Heidi made a note in my file, then flipped it shut. "Take a seat outside in the waiting room, please."

Was that it? No questions? No interview? No chance to let my personality shine through? I studied their faces for a sign—the tiniest hint that they liked me—but their expressions were blank.

"Thanks for your time," I said, but half of the reps had already disappeared back in their offices.

Out in the reception area, I settled into a gilded pink chair for more excruciating waiting. On the sofa across from me, two lanky models were talking in low voices. I picked up a magazine, but I was too nervous to read.

"That job was great," the redhead said. Her hair was long and tapered around her face. "Did you see the shot the photographer got of me in that cape? It was like, half a mile long. I've got it in my portfolio."

"That *was* a fun shoot," said the brunette, a thin girl with a short pixie haircut. "Not like the last ad I shot. It was for one of those sports drinks, and they wanted to get me sweating. Of course, I don't sweat, so they had to keep spraying me with cold water. Needless to say, I was *not* happy. So I just stood there, calculating how much money I was making a second."

The two models started giggling. "I do that too!" the redhead cried. "Especially if they make me wear ugly clothes."

I glanced at them, then back at the magazine. Obviously these girls weren't here for the open call. They were already with the agency. I was sure that the brunette was the model in the perfume ad in front of me. How many ads had they done? These girls had gotten some major work. For modeling, Diamond was the place to be. God, I had to get in. A few modeling gigs a year, and I could probably earn what I needed for college. That's where Mom had it wrong. This wasn't about ethics or ego. It was about money.

"Kerri Hopkins?"

I was so tuned into the models' conversation I didn't even notice the older woman standing at the reception desk until she called my name. I stood up and recognized her face. She was one of the reps who'd watched me walk. "I'm Jane Katz," she said as we shook hands. "Let's go into my office."

Following her through the maze of cubes, I studied her shoes—low platforms. Her skirt—wool. Her jacket—something tweedy. There were white streaks throughout her brown hair, but Jane didn't really seem old.

Her office was a real office with a small window and a waxy looking plant and a whole wall of print ads popping with daring, sultry models. And I wanted to be among them. I pictured myself in a splashy photo—a whole series of ads—and Jane Katz was cutting them out, telling me that the best decision she'd ever made was choosing to take me on as a model.

"Have a seat," Ms. Katz said, jarring me out of my fantasy.

I sat in one of the chairs opposite her desk and tried my best to appear enthusiastic without sucking up.

"I have to be honest with, Kerri. We haven't decided about you yet."

A knife in my heart. But it wasn't hopeless.

"Half of the agents like you," she explained, "but the other half are not so sure. So my idea is that we enter you in a modeling contest at Marshall Fields."

"Really?" I smiled, feeling genuine enthusiasm this time.

"The only drawback is that the contest is tomorrow," Jane went on. "We know it's short notice, but there is a slot, and it would give us a chance to really assess your skills."

She rested her chin in one hand and tapped a manicured finger against her cheek. She was studying me, and the message was clear. This contest was a test.

"Tomorrow . . ." The senior trip schedule danced in my mind. I couldn't remember what was planned, but I knew it was going to be a problem to sneak off again. How could I get away from the teachers without getting caught?

"Interested?" Jane prodded.

"Well, I'm on this school trip, and—"

"I see," Jane said, closing my folder. "Well, it was nice—"

"No, no, I didn't mean I couldn't go," I insisted. "What does the contest require? I mean, what do I have to do?"

Jane tapped her pen against the folder and rattled off the details. "Each girl will model two outfits—one sportswear and one couture. All wardrobe, choreography, makeup, and hairstyling will be provided by Marshall Fields. Contestants will be judged on appearance, poise, and how well their personality shines through on the runway."

I tried to process the information as quickly as she said it. The contest sounded so professional. This was even more exciting than today's interview.

She brought her pen up to her chin, looking bored. "So, will you grace us with your presence or not?"

"Absolutely," I said quickly. "I can get there; no problem." Big lie. But somehow I'd have to figure out how to make another great escape.

Chapter 9

Jessica

Dear Jessica,

For the first time in my life I've agreed to throw a wild and crazy party. But how do I make it fun without getting myself into major trouble? More important, how do I stop FREAKING OUT?

I didn't have the answers. All I had were my lists. In my left jeans pocket were the things I needed to do before the party. In the right, were the people I wanted to invite.

I pulled out my guest list, and checked it. So far there were nineteen names, but I knew more would crop up once I showed the list to my friends. *Oh, God,* I thought feeling another wave of serious freak out creeping up on me. *Cut it out,* I told myself. *No matter what, you're limiting this party to no more than twenty-five people. Everything will be fine.* I figured we could squeeze that many kids into my room, with eight on each bed, three on the windowsill, etc.

I shoved the paper back in my pocket. At the moment we were working off my To Do list. Kerri had already gone to the modeling agency, but Erin, Maya, and I were collecting ice buckets from the kids we knew.

"You realize you're crazy," Maya said as she followed me down the hall of our floor. I knocked on the door to Amber's room and waited.

"No answer," I said, trying to change the subject. I was worried enough on my own. I didn't need Maya to remind me of all the things that could go wrong. I held up the ice buckets I'd already collected from other students. "I've got six and you've got two."

"And I've got eight," Erin called from down the hall. She carried a stack of ice buckets tucked under her chin. "A lot of kids on the eighth floor hadn't gone to breakfast yet."

"Would you listen to me, Jess?" Maya said, following me to the next door. "If you get caught, you're going to be in big trouble. We're talking end of trip, possible suspension from school. You might even get kicked out of the university program."

"Don't even *say* that," I said. I knew this whole party thing was risky, but I couldn't think about that now. I had to be organized. I had to be focused if I really wanted to pull this thing off. And I did. I really did.

"But it's possible," Maya went on. "And if you throw a big party in this hotel, your chances of getting caught are excellent."

"It's going to be a small party," I insisted, knocking on another door. "No more than twenty-five kids. How noisy could that be?" I hoped that sounded confident.

"Even if it's loud, we've got a good buffer zone," Erin pointed out. "There are students on the floors above and below us. Nobody's going to complain."

"And if nobody complains, nobody's going to find out about the party." I handed two of my ice buckets to Maya and knocked again.

The door opened, and Kathleen Karpinski peered out at me.

"Party tonight in my room. Starts after curfew." I pointed inside the room. "Give us your ice bucket, and bring some munchies when you come."

"Cool!" She disappeared, and I could hear her telling her roommate about the party. She returned with the ice bucket, which I added to my stash. "See you tonight," she said, then the door closed.

"This is making me very nervous," Maya said.

"Don't you see that I have to do this?" I replied. "This is enough for now. Let's dump these in the room and grab some breakfast. After that, we've just got to work out the drinks. We can get ice tonight. And we can make sure the rest of the kids on the list get invited during today's trip." That seemed to cover it. Maybe this party thing was simpler than it seemed.

Maya followed behind me. "If this is about the Truth or Dare game, you don't have to—"

"That's not it," I interrupted. "It's more than that. I'm sick of being the good girl. This is my chance to show people what I'm really like. It's time for me to break a few rules."

"Yes!" Erin dropped her stack of ice buckets to the floor and gave me a high five. "Deep inside, I always knew you had the potential to be crazy," she said. "Welcome to the team."

I felt good about that. At least Erin was supporting me. This party was really going to happen. And I was going to make sure it was stupendous if it killed me. I turned to Maya. "Please, don't jinx this for me."

Maya juggled her stack of ice buckets. "I'd never do that, Jess. I'm behind you, completely. I just want to make sure you know what you're doing."

"That's why I made up these lists," I said. "Everything's under control." *I think,* I added silently.

We rode the elevator to our room, dropped off the buckets, and headed downstairs to the breakfast buffet. As I slid pancakes and bacon onto my plate, two seniors I really didn't know walked over to me.

"Is it true about the after-curfew party?" one girl asked.

I nodded, trying to appear calm despite the fact that I didn't even know these kids. They weren't on my list, but I figured I'd have to add them on. Two more people wasn't a big deal, right? "Price of admission is one food item," I told them.

"Cool." They smiled, and I walked away.

Maya hurried over to me, juggling an apple and a bowl of oatmeal. "All the seniors from the girls' track team are coming," she said as we spotted Erin at a table. We headed over to join her, and I pulled out my guest list.

"*All* of them?" I repeated, wondering how many that was.

"Yeah. Three," she said.

I let out the breath I didn't even know I was holding until now. I added the three names, along with the other two mystery seniors. "That's twenty-four," I said. "We're getting close to my limit." And I didn't want to go over it.

"You can add two more," Erin said. "I just ran into a bunch of kids from the theater department. They're in."

And I'm over my limit, I thought. *But just by one. That isn't so bad. Things are still under control.* I bit into a piece of crispy bacon.

"Hey, Jess," Erin asked. "So how are we going to smuggle a dozen cases of soda up to our room without attracting attention? What's the plan?"

The plan? I had sodas on the list, but I hadn't considered a method of transport. Why hadn't I thought of a plan? I willed myself not to freak. *Get a grip, Jess. Think positively. Deep breath.*

Okay. I did the only logical, organized, focused thing I could think of. I pulled out my To Do list and added one more thing: *Get a plan—fast.*

Kerri

By the time I got back to the hotel and called Maya on her cell phone, the class was through with the tour of Shedd Aquarium, where they'd also grabbed lunch. "We're just getting on the busses to go on the river cruise," Maya said. "The boat leaves from the Michigan Avenue Bridge."

"Got it," I said, feeling sort of strange to be back at the hotel while everyone else was out. The bed beckoned, and for a second I wondered if I should change my plans and catch a nap. No. I couldn't risk it. I was already pushing my luck. "I'll see you at the bridge," I told Maya. "And what about the teachers?"

"No one noticed. They took attendance on the bus, but when Mr. Calvert called out your name, Luke said 'Here' in a high voice. We all laughed, but I saw that Mr. Calvert just marked you present."

I was off the hook, at least for today. As soon as we said good-bye I rushed to change into jeans, then hurried downstairs. The man at the desk told me to take a bus straight down Michigan Avenue, and I made it to the bridge in no time. I found a little souvenir shop to wait in, so the teachers wouldn't see me standing by the boat. When the buses pulled up and started to unload, I stepped out and joined the mass of kids.

"Kerri!" Matt called as he stepped off the bus.

I cut through the crowd and took his hand. "Shh!" I whispered in his ear. "Don't make a big scene." Ms. Gomes was ahead of us, making arrangements with the dock master. The other teachers stood at the doors of the buses.

Erin, Maya, and Jessica got off the bus behind

Matt. "How did it go?" Erin asked.

"Great, I think. I'm not in yet, but they want me to be in a modeling contest. Get this, Maya—it's at Marshall Fields. I have to be there tomorrow at eleven for rehearsal."

Maya's eyes lit up. "My shrine!"

"That's awesome, Kerri." Jessica beamed.

"Really great!" Matt pulled me into his arms for a hug, then started to dance me up the gangplank onto the boat.

I stiffened, catching sight of the big double-decker boat for the first time. I flashed back to my nightmare. It gave me the creeps. "Hold on," I told Matt, staring at the deck.

"What's wrong?" Matt asked.

Kids were pushing past us up the ramp. I really didn't want to go aboard, but it seemed ridiculous to let a dream stop me. Yeah, like the teachers would really buy that excuse. "I . . . I'll tell you later," I told Matt, taking his hand. We walked onto the boat, right past Ms. Gomes.

"We're thrilled for you," Erin said, staring at Ms. Gomes, who didn't seem to be listening to our conversation. "And you know what? I think we have the afternoon free tomorrow."

"We do," Luke said. "So you're in the clear, Kerri."

"I hope you guys can come watch," I said, trying to sound enthusiastic. This boat thing really threw me into a slight panic. I was still holding on to Matt's hand with no intention of letting go. "Jane, the Diamond rep, told me anyone can attend the show. They're trying to attract shoppers."

"Count me in," Maya said.

"Me too," Jessica said. "Forget everything I said about that permission slip. This really seems to be working out for you."

Matt pulled me closer and pulled our joined hands up to his chest. "You know I wouldn't miss it."

I looked into his eyes, wishing these other people would disappear so I could tell him all about the nightmare.

Amber Brawley came over and grabbed Jessica's arm. "The party is open, right? Because we met some exchange students at the Aquarium, and they might be able to come."

Jessica looked around as if the answer was hanging in the air, then nodded. "Yeah, sure. But how many kids?"

"Four," Amber said. "I'll make sure they bring food and everything."

Jess nodded as Amber walked away. "That makes twenty-eight." She smiled slightly, but I could tell she was a little worried about the people count. "Well, I guess we can manage. I mean, everyone probably won't be in the room at the same time, right?"

"So, how's that party planning going?" I asked Jess.

"Great," Jessica said. "I've covered just about everything on my list. Just a few more people to invite, in case they haven't gotten the word. Right now the only thing left is figuring out the drinks. I haven't come up with a teacher-proof way to get enough soda for about thirty people up to the room."

Erin snapped her fingers. "There's Wolfie Tanner over by the rail." Wolfie was a hulking senior. "Maybe the wrestling squad will carry the soda up in the service elevator."

"Do you think?" Jessica's eyebrows lifted.

"Let's ask him," Erin prodded, giving Jess a push. They disappeared into the crowd, with Glen following Erin.

"Welcome aboard!" said a male voice coming out of a loudspeaker. "As soon as the captain pushes off, we'll be ready to begin our tour of some of the finest buildings in the world, sponsored by the Chicago Architectural Foundation. . . ."

Luke and Maya went off to find a seat, and I

grabbed Matt's hand and pulled him over to a half-empty bench. I needed to get that dream off my mind.

"You okay?" he asked. "I thought you were going to pull me right off the ship back there. If I didn't know any better, I'd think you were afraid of boats."

"You're right." I bit my lip. He knew me so well. "I didn't want to get on," I admitted. "Matt, I had this horrible dream last night. You and I were on a boat, and . . ." I paused, calculating for a second. Telling Matt about the wedding part was bound to freak him out. "We were on a boat together, and I was a famous model, but the boat began to sink. And you jumped off and swam away, but my gown was soaked and I was stuck there. Alone on the boat—with Donna. Can you believe it? She was in my dream."

He shook his head. "That's some nightmare," he said. "No wonder you were freaked at getting on the boat."

I nodded, starting to feel better. "I couldn't stop thinking about it. All morning I could see the look on her face. . . . I was drowning, and . . . and she was happy about it. Smiling . . ." I shook my head. "It's like she's still after me. I know that doesn't make sense, but—"

"You're still scared," Matt said. "And that's understandable. The girl tried to run you down with her car, Kerri. But that's all over. And even better, Donna is hundreds of miles away from us, back in Madison."

"You're right," I said, leaning against him. "I'm safe here."

"Forget about Donna," Matt said as our boat passed under a low, arched bridge. "Promise me you won't let her ruin our time together."

Matt was right. Donna had done enough damage. "I'm going to try to put her out of my mind," I promised.

"You know," Matt said, cradling my hand in both of his, "I've got good news too."

"What?" I smiled, though I was really drawing a blank. Then he reached into his pocket and pulled out two tickets.

"The Gaylord concert!" I said. "You got them."

His eyes glimmered with pride. "The concert was completely sold out, but they had a cancellation while I was there. Can you believe it? That's when I knew it was meant to be."

"Awesome," I said. "What night are they for?"

"Tomorrow at eight."

My blood went cold. The modeling contest was scheduled to run until at least nine or ten at night. Hadn't I just told everybody that? No. I hadn't. I just told them I had to be at Marshall Fields at eleven. But that was only for rehearsal. The actual judging began around six o'clock. I stared at Matt, wondering how I was going to break it to him.

"Tomorrow?" My voice cracked a little, revealing my panic.

"I know, I'm wigged out about it too. I mean, the tickets were really expensive, but then I thought, hey, it's our chance to be together alone, and the music will blow us away. So I went for it."

"But, Matt . . ." I had to tell him that this was a problem. "I don't know if—"

"Don't worry about the price," he interrupted. "You're worth it." He put his arm around me and nuzzled my ear. "*We're* worth it."

I closed my eyes, trying to sort this thing out. I should just tell him I couldn't do it. But this concert was so important to him, and I had already canceled on the Breakfast Club.

What could I say? *Matt, I want to go with you, but I can't. . . .*

"This is our chance to be alone together," Matt said, squeezing my hand. I squeezed back, but it killed me to think I was going to disappoint him. "We'll go to dinner first—maybe to the House of

Blues. And wait till you see where these seats are. They're right by the stage."

He was *so* psyched, and I was so not going to be there.

If only I could be in two places at once. . . .

Chapter 10

Jessica

The cruise was only half over, but the boat was buzzing with talk of my party. I guess good news travels fast, and for once, my name was in the headline.

"I'm definitely in," said Sidney Townsend, the head cheerleader. "And I know Angie is too. Do you have someone doing music?"

"I haven't gotten to that yet," I told Sidney, "but I will." It was on my party-planning list, and I was hot on Wolfie's heels. Planning a party the Carvelli way. Sure, I had delegated a few things to Maya and Erin, but I was in control. Maya was in charge of music. The ice was covered. I was going to recruit Wolfie to lug up soda. I'd even gotten Erin to wheedle some information out of Mr. Calvert. It turned out the teachers were planning an outing of their own after curfew. Some dinner with an old friend. Bye-bye, curfew police.

"Jessica, what are you waiting for?" Sidney asked. "Music is key."

"I'm on top of it, Sidney," I said, scribbling the two cheerleaders' names onto my guest list. That made thirty people—now, *that* was my absolute limit. I turned away, searching for Wolfie.

He wasn't by the rail. I scanned the rows of faces for my friends and accidentally bumped into Ms. Gomes, who was directing foot traffic.

"Sorry," I said as she glared at me. Then I crossed to the other side of the ship, on my mission.

"Before we look at individual buildings," a voice boomed over the loudspeaker, "you should know why Chicago came to be an architectural center. It started with the devastating Chicago fire of 1871. When the smoke cleared, much of the city needed to be completely rebuilt—"

"There she is!" Angie shouted. "Jess! Over here."

I went over to Angie, who was talking to some guys I didn't know. "I was just telling them about your party," she said. "After curfew, and everybody's going."

Everybody? I thought. Not quite. Just a select few. And these guys weren't on my list. I was already up to thirty kids. I couldn't add any more to the party. *Not one person!*

"What's the room number?" one of the guys asked.

"It's not—"

"Twelve thirty-three," Angie answered brightly. "I hope you can come."

"Yeah, we'll be there," one of the guys answered before I could uninvite them.

I plunked onto a bench, and did a quick head count. Four more guys made *thirty-four*. How was I supposed to fit thirty-four people in my room?

"Psst! Jessica!" I turned to see Sidney sliding onto the bench beside me. A kid with a backward baseball cap stood over us, chewing gum with rapid motion. "I talked to Jimmy about the music. Do you know each other?"

He shrugged. I shook my head. I'd delegated the music to Maya, but figured I could take care of it now if Jimmy was interested.

"Jimmy Wright. He's got a portable CD player that he's going to let us use."

"Us?" I blinked at Sidney. Since when did it become her party?

"I'm not lending it out," Jimmy jumped in. "I'll be the deejay, that's the deal."

"Shh!" someone called from behind us, apparently trying to hear the tour guide.

"Okay, Jimmy," I said, thinking fast. "You be

deejay, and if you take care of the music we'll waive your admission fee." *And that makes you guest number thirty-five,* I added silently. *Oh, God.*

"Really?" He seemed impressed. I guess he hadn't heard that the price for admission was just a bag of chips. "That's a deal. What's the room number?"

"Twelve thirty-three," someone called out. It was another girl I didn't know, who laughed when I turned toward her. "After-curfew party. We're all going," she said.

You're not invited! I wanted to shout. But I didn't. A, it would have alerted the teachers to my party. And B, it would have made me look like a world-class jerk.

I counted her group of friends. Four girls total. That made thirty-nine people. *Thirty-nine!*

I wanted to blurt out an excuse as to why I suddenly had to cancel my party—I had to wash my hair, I was feeling sick . . . *any*thing. But who was I kidding? I knew it was way too late to back out of this. So instead, I gave Jimmy the details, and he and Sidney disappeared.

Now it was time to find my friends. But as I turned, I spotted Wolfie Tanner hanging near the railing. I tapped him on the arm. He ran a hand over his short, spiked hair as I introduced myself.

"Yeah." He pointed at me. "You're the Jessica who's having the party."

"Right. And I need your help." I explained about how we needed to cart the cases of soda into the hotel. "Do you think you could get a bunch of guys from the wrestling team to take them up in the elevator?"

He twisted his face, considering it. "I'd like to help you out, but if we get caught setting up a party we'll get in big trouble. And we've got a big meet coming up next week."

"No way!" I said. "I was sure you'd help us out, Wolfie."

"Look, I'm sorry," he said, "but we can't risk it. Some of us are already on probation for hanging Sean Hill's jockey shorts from the school flagpole." Wolfie walked off to join his friend, then turned back.

"Don't worry," Wolfie told me. "I'll still be there with my buds."

I stared at him and his very large friends. *Gulp.* "How many?"

"Five. Six with me."

"Okay," I said. That meant forty-five. I tried to convince myself that I could still handle this. That it was still under control. Party Carvelli-style . . . Oh, God.

Don't panic, Jessica, I reminded myself. *Do NOT panic.*

"Jess!" Erin called. Maya was with her. "Did you find Wolfie?"

"Yeah, and he said no."

"No way!" Erin said.

"That's not the only thing. The party guests are up in the mid-forties."

"Whoa," Maya said. "This is going to be huge."

"Yeah," I muttered. "Too many guests, and nothing to drink." I didn't want to seem nervous, but I couldn't help it. And though, I told myself not to . . . I *was* beginning to panic. Okay, not beginning. I was in full-fledged, Jessica Carvelli freak-out mode. Big time.

"Don't worry," Maya told me. "I have an idea."

I turned toward her, my curiosity piqued.

"Hey, when your father is in politics, you have to pick up a few tips." I shook my head, still not following. She slung her arm around my shoulders. "Jessica, we've got some shopping to do. It's cheap, it's big, and it's very accommodating. Stop for a moment and consider the beauty of the punch bowl."

"I still don't understand how the punch bowl plan got us to Marshall Fields," I said as we rode up on the escalator to the third floor. While the guys had headed off to see if they could catch a tour of Wrigley Field, Maya, Kerri, Erin, and I had hopped on the El to the world-famous department store.

"It's simple," Maya said. "We can get cheap plastic punch bowls at any party store, but we can't walk into the hotel with bags that say PARTY GIANT or something, right? So we're here to get those big, Marshall Fields shopping bags with nice handles. They'll be perfect for stashing the stuff we need for the party and sneaking it into the hotel."

"And the bonus for Maya is, that to get the shopping bags, we have to *buy* things," Erin explained.

"Exactly," Maya said. "You guys know I've been dying to get over here. Should we start in sportswear or shoes?"

Erin stepped off the escalator ahead of me and pointed to a zebra print dress. "This floor looks good."

"Just make it quick," I said, checking my watch. "We still have to get the punch ingredients and set up."

"Don't worry," Maya told me. "I've helped my dad throw dozens of parties. And I've perfected the art of punch-making. It's a snap."

Kerri and I lingered behind, and I could tell she

had something on her mind. "You're too quiet. What's going on?"

Her lips tightened into a thin line. "I've messed up things with Matt again, only he doesn't know it yet."

"Well, then you didn't screw it up yet, right?" I said, trying to cheer her up.

She leaned on a rack of red wool dresses and stared at the floor. "I promised him I'd go to the Duke Gaylord concert, and he's really into it. But he got tickets for tomorrow night, and the contest is scheduled to go on into the evening."

"Ouch." That was a tough one. "Maybe he can change the night of the tickets."

Kerri shook her head. "Everything is sold out."

"That *is* a problem," I said, feeling sorry for her. "What are you going to do?"

"What *can* I do?" Kerri said quietly. I noticed her usual sparkle was missing.

"I hate to say it, but you don't look so hot."

She pulled back her hair and groaned. "I barely slept last night. I . . . I don't know."

"Kerri," I said, gently. "What is it?"

She glanced away. "Nothing. Forget it."

"I may be obsessed with party planning, but I'm still conscious enough to see that you're upset. What happened?"

"It was just a weird dream. Kept me up most of the night."

"About what?" I asked.

Kerri shook her head. "It was stupid, Jess. Just forget it."

"Oh. Okay," I said. I knew when not to push Kerri for details.

Maya popped over to us, holding up two sweaters. "Look at these, marked down twice. I can't decide between the colors," she said, disappearing again.

"So get both," Erin's voice rose from behind a stack of sweaters. "Your dad won't care."

"You're right," Maya said, "and I'll ask for *two* bags."

Maya bought the sweaters, along with a pair of shoes and a leather hobo sack. Within a half hour we were riding the escalators down, past bright displays of sweaters and sparkling perfume bottles.

"How many bags did we end up with?" I asked lifting a shopping bag.

"Six!" Maya said proudly. "That last sales clerk gave me two extras."

"It *is* a fabulous store," Kerri said as the escalator swept us past a wall of sparkling silver settings. "I can't wait for the contest tomorrow. I've got a really good feeling about this."

"So you're not going to ditch the contest for Matt?" I asked. "Good."

"What?" Erin's mouth dropped open.

But Kerri was already shaking her head. "I wouldn't. I couldn't. It's too big an opportunity."

"What's this about Matt?" Maya prodded.

"It's that jazz concert." Kerri went onto explain her dilemma as we left the store and headed toward the train.

I tuned her out as we walked down the street, and started going through my mental list for the party. Ice—got it at the hotel. Punch bowls. Cups. Ladles. Juice concentrate. Ginger ale. Oh, and sherbet. How much was all of this going to cost? All the girls had agreed to chip in ten dollars each, and Maya was sure that would cover it.

Carvelli party list nearly completed. Good.

As we started climbing the stairs to the El, a train above us was leaving the station and passengers streamed down around us. A tall girl with long, dark hair twisted into a French braid came down the stairs, her hand sliding along the far railing. Her eyes were fixed on the steps.

I did a double take. She looked exactly like my sister, Lisa. But Lisa went to Marquette University in Wisconsin. What would she be doing in Chicago?

She passed us, continuing down the stairs. I

paused on a step and turned around. She looked *exactly* like her. Even walked like her. "Lisa?" I said.

And the girl turned around. The recognition in her eyes was unmistakable.

It *was* my sister.

Chapter 11

"**L**isa!" I ran down the stairs. She was waiting on the landing, other commuters moving past her. There was something strange about the way she didn't smile or even meet me halfway. She didn't seem happy to see me. Actually, she looked nervous, her dark eyes flitting from me to my friends on the stairs above.

"Hey, Lisa!" Kerri called.

Lisa waved, still not smiling. "What are you doing here?" she asked me as I jumped down to the landing.

"Senior trip," I said. "The real question is, what are you doing here?"

"Me?" She seemed surprised. "I'm here on a road trip with friends—just a quick one."

"That's wild!" I said. "I mean, that we're here at the same time. I can't believe Mom didn't say anything to me."

"Mom doesn't know," Lisa said quickly, a guarded look on her face. "And I really have to go. My . . . my friends are waiting."

"Oh." I felt a little hurt that she was brushing me off so quickly. "Okay. Where are you staying?"

"With . . . with a friend." She looked away, and suddenly I realized that there was more to this story than Lisa was letting on. She was hiding something. "Look, Jess, I've got to run."

"No, wait! Maybe we can get together," I said.

"I'm really busy," she replied, turning away. "I'll see you when I come home. Uh, maybe for spring break or something." She continued down the stairs, not even looking back.

"Take care!" I called.

She turned back for another quick wave, then disappeared through the street exit.

I stood there, thinking for a second about how Lisa was not her usual self. Since she'd left for college we'd kind of bonded over the phone. I'd been moaning to her for months about Alex, and she'd never complained. She gave great relationship advice, and I'd needed a lot of it. But today, that bond was barely there. The air had been thick with something . . . tension. Or maybe it was secrecy.

"Well, that was weird," I said, joining my friends.

"What is she doing here?" Erin asked.

"She said something about a road trip." As we reached the platform I heard the rumble of the train pulling in. There was a mad rush to pay our tokens, push through the turnstiles, and tote our bags into a car.

Once there, I held onto a pole still puzzled by Lisa. "Did you notice?" I asked, thinking aloud. "She didn't seem happy to see me at all. And she said Mom doesn't know she's here. Why wouldn't she tell Mom she was coming to Chicago?"

"Why should she tell your mom?" Erin pointed out. "It's not like she needs permission."

Kerri nudged closer to the pole as someone passed behind her. "And college kids don't tell their parents every little detail," she added.

"I guess you're right." The car doors opened at the next stop. "It's not like I'm about to tell my parents about this party either."

"Exactly," Erin said as we stepped off the train and onto the platform, ready to buy the rest of the things on my list.

"I can't believe this is all coming together," I said, walking down the street with a backpack filled with cartons of sherbet, and a shopping bag with cans of juice concentrate. We'd finished our shopping and were headed back to the hotel. "All because of a stupid round of Truth or Dare."

"As my mom says, you don't know what you can accomplish till you try," Erin told us as we crossed the street to our hotel. "Of course, I know she wasn't talking about an after-curfew party, but it *does* apply."

We laughed. I felt like skipping, but I didn't want the heavy shopping bag I was holding nor the cold, lumpy backpack banging against me. Besides, skipping into the hotel would totally reinforce the Goody Two-shoes image I was trying to lose.

Kerri held open the wide double doors, and we stepped into the hotel.

"Just a couple of girls, back with their purchases," Maya said, giggling.

"Would you relax?" Erin said under her breath. "Don't make a big deal out of it."

"Right," I said, trying to radiate a coolness I didn't quite feel. I started walking across the lobby, scanning the guests and pretending to be casual. I glanced at the sofa off to the side of the reservations, and my breath caught in my throat.

Mr. Calvert and Ms. Gomes. What were they doing down here? A whole city to explore, and they had to stake out the hotel lobby?

I felt my face growing warm. I knew I was

blushing. "Don't look now," I said to Erin, "but the teachers are down here."

"Stay cool," Erin reminded me. "And look them right in the eye. They won't catch us . . . we have shopping bags, that's it."

"Right," I said, still feeling a little shaky. Kerri and Maya were already passing right in front of them, saying hello. Nodding. Scurrying ahead to the elevator with their Marshall Fields bags in tow.

No problem, I thought, pushing on. A juice can clinked against the punch bowl in my bag, and I pretended not to care. I smiled at Mr. Calvert and noticed that Ms. Gomes was talking to another man. Then I moved ahead. *Phew, I made it!*

"Jessica?" Mr. Calvert called after me.

I froze, more aware than ever of the party goods I was carrying.

"Jessica," he called again.

I had to turn around and look at him, but as I did I felt sure he could read the guilty expression on my face.

"Can I speak to you a moment?" My heart sank to my toes as he waved me over, with a wave that wasn't friendly or warm, but formal, businesslike.

Oh, God, I thought miserably. *They know about the party.*

Chapter 12

Biting my lip, I plodded over to Mr. Calvert and Ms. Gomes. A mirror with an elaborately carved frame hung behind the couch they were sitting on, and I cringed when I caught sight of my own guilty expression. Red cheeks. Lowered head. Wrinkled shopping bag, containing three huge punch bowls and ten cans of frozen juice concentrate, clanging against my leg.

"We've been waiting for you," Mr. Calvert said.

It's over, I thought. *I've blown the entire party!*

I wasn't sure who the man talking to Ms. Gomes was, but I suspected he was with hotel security. I was *so* busted.

"I wanted to introduce you to Professor Earle," Mr. Calvert said, gesturing to the man beside him. "He teaches at NYU."

Professor Earle, a middle-aged man with thick eyebrows and dark hair, leaned forward to shake my hand. I had to transfer the shopping bag to my left hand, which I did with a thump and a clang.

"Jessica is hoping to attend NYU in the fall," Mr. Calvert went on.

I nodded like an idiot. Was that what this was about? Just helping me connect with an NYU professor? Actually, it all made sense. This was probably the man all the teachers were dining with after curfew. God bless Professor Earle.

"What do you want to major in?" Professor Earle asked.

Criminal mischief, I thought. "Journalism," I said. "Or maybe communications. I love to write."

"Jessica started out as a yearbook editor this year," Mr. Calvert said. "But she's had to scale down her high school duties since she's already taking some classes at the University of Wisconsin. She's at the top of her class."

A world-class deviate.

"That's impressive," the professor said.

I smiled, thinking how Mr. Calvert was singing my praises, while I was trying to sneak past him with contraband. Ironic. And it made me feel even weirder. I guessed my conscience was way too heavy for me to lead a life of crime.

"Professor Earle teaches economics," Ms. Gomes said. "Which is hard to believe, since he failed math when we were in fifth grade together."

The professor waved her off. "That wasn't about math; that was about Miss Graves favoring all the girls." They both laughed, and I could see they were still good friends. Professor Earle changed the subject. "What kind of writing do you do?" he asked me.

"Fiction," I answered, "but I'm open to lots of things. I just got a job writing an online advice column for teens."

"Excellent," the professor said, nodding. "Sounds like you're very ambitious."

I nodded, glancing straight down into the shopping bag. My back was now frozen from the sherbet, and I had to move from one foot to another to keep from shivering.

"We'll let you go," Ms. Gomes said. "Looks like you've been busy shopping."

"Very busy," I said, lifting the bag. "Well, nice meeting you."

"Look me up when you get to NYU," the professor called after me.

Without turning back I marched over to the elevator where my friends were waiting, mystified.

"That was so close," I mumbled.

"You're telling *me*," Erin said, pulling me into the elevator. "But you survived, unscathed."

"And free to party," I said. "Just as soon as I get this frozen pack off my back!"

Both excitement and fear welled inside me as we rode the elevator up and barreled into my room. We flung down the bags and tried to sort through them and organize.

"This place is a mess," Erin said, kicking an empty plastic bag aside.

"I know, I know," I said, feeling another twinge of panic. The party was going to start in two hours, and nothing was in the right place. And we all had to take showers and get ready too.

"You need somewhere to put the punch bowls," Kerri said, walking over to the low dresser. It was covered with stuff Erin and I had brought—bottles of nail polish, foundation, perfume, and two hair dryers. Kerri grabbed an empty shopping bag and scooped everything off the desk. Eyebrow pencils and compacts clanked together as they dropped into the bag.

"Hey, watch the makeup!" Erin cried.

"Finito." Kerri wiped down the dresser with some toilet paper and set a punch bowl on top.

"If we move the phone, we can set another one up on the night stand," I said, tossing the notepad and pen into the drawer.

"And I'll bet one of our neighbors would be

cool about letting the party extend into their room," Erin said.

"You can use ours," Kerri offered.

"Thanks, but you have the modeling contest tomorrow," I pointed out. "You have to get to bed at a decent hour. Besides, you're a few doors down. Let's see if we can get a volunteer from next door."

I went next door and talked to Ginny Torres, a track runner who was rooming with Sarah Driscoll. They seemed a little hesitant at first, but when I mentioned that a lot of guys were coming, Ginny talked Sarah into having a punch bowl in their room.

"We'll be back to set everything up as soon as curfew check is over," I told them.

Back in my room, my friends had straightened up the worst of the mess.

"Looks good," I said. "We can mix the punch in the bathroom, then move it out as soon as curfew check is over."

"Let's get dressed first," Maya said. "I'm actually going to have a chance to wear one of my new sweaters—the black one with the bell-cut sleeves."

"Well, I'm trying out a sheer cape that I made from my mom's old curtains," Erin said. "It's white, but I'm wearing my fuchsia camisole underneath.

Completely decadent."

I opened the closet and took a hot pink sweater out of my suitcase. It wasn't fancy, but it showed off my figure well. "That color is great on you," Maya said as she headed toward the door. "See you in a bit!"

"Not till after curfew check," I reminded her. "Don't want to make Ms. Gomes suspicious."

We showered quickly and threw ourselves together. "It's not easy digging makeup out of a shopping bag," Erin said, leaning toward the mirror to coast her lashes with mascara.

"Things will be back to normal tomorrow," I promised. "But thanks for giving up the room for tonight. I mean, thanks for going for it."

"For the party of the millennium?" Erin smiled at me in the mirror. "How could I say no?"

I had just finished drying my hair when a sharp knock sounded on the door. Erin pulled it open, and Ms. Gomes peeked in.

"How's everything?" she asked.

"Just fine," I said, leaning out of the bathroom.

"Have a good night," she called, closing the door.

I waved at the closed door. "Don't hurry back, Ms. Gomes!"

After that, Jimmy Wright was the first to show

up. "Hey, where do I set up the music?" he asked, smacking his gum.

We decided to put him near the window, so he could set up his speakers in the corner. He was doing a sound check, dancing with himself in front of the mirror when Maya and Kerri returned.

"Sounds like a party to me," Kerri said.

"Do you think so?" I dug my nails into the palms of my hands, still nervous about pulling the whole thing off. I checked the clock. Eleven thirty already. "We'd better mix the punch."

Maya showed me how to mix up the punch—concentrate, water, ginger ale, and sherbet. I poured myself a cup to test it. "It's good!"

"Don't look so surprised," Maya said. "I told you I've made punch before."

We were still mixing the second batch when the first people showed up—Amber Brawley and some of the student government crew.

"Here's my ticket." Amber tossed me a bag of Cheetos, which I poured into an ice bucket. Her friends had brought Oreos and pretzels. Within minutes there were six kids sitting on the bed, munching, drinking, and rocking to the music. Then the wrestling team came, led by Wolfie, who helped us get all the heavy punch bowls in position. Then came a bunch of kids I didn't know, but I didn't care about the head count anymore.

The party was really starting . . . and I was ready to rock!

Kerri

I danced across the corridor, my eyes on Matt. I was so crazy about him. How could I break the news that was going to hurt him?

"Jess really knows how to throw a party," Matt shouted as we both moved to the music that thumped out into the hall from Jessica's room. "Who knew that sweet little Jess had it in her?"

I did. Having known Jessica since babyhood, I knew she wasn't the straight arrow kids had pegged her to be. But I didn't say that to Matt, not with the noise level thrumming around us. Instead, I smiled, swaying to the beat as other kids danced around us in the corridor. The party had spilled down the hall, way past the room next door, but so far no one had complained. Maybe this really was Jess's lucky night.

And my *un*lucky night. I still hadn't come up with a way to tell Matt that I had to bail on the concert. And with each minute that went by, I felt more and more guilty.

The music ended, and Matt grabbed me by the

arms and pulled me back as the crowd billowed toward us.

"What's going on?" I asked, suddenly pressed against the wall.

"Some kind of event," Matt said.

Kids lined the two walls, making way for a group of guys at the end of the corridor. With a deep roar, they came stomping toward us in teams of two—the rear guy holding the front guy's legs while he pawed the ground for a wheelbarrow race. I recognized Wolfie Tanner and Armand Sinanian from the wrestling squad, as well as Turtle Donovan from the football team.

"Go, Turtle!" Matt shouted, routing on his teammate.

I had to laugh. "Wheelbarrow races? What's next, duck, duck, goose?"

"Hey, it's a race," Matt said emphatically. "Go, man!"

The competitors pounded down the hall, the crowd closing behind them so we couldn't see who won.

"Next heat!" someone called. "This time, girls only!"

"Cool." Matt squeezed my shoulders. "Are you in?"

"Nah. I'd better save myself for tomorrow."

"Good idea." He pulled me around so that he was leaning on the wall and I was leaning on him. "Is that what's bothering you tonight?" he asked. "The competition?"

I had to look away. How could I tell him the truth, that I was going to have to blow our big date tomorrow night? "I don't know," I said. "I guess I'm just worried. Lacking sleep. Still freaked about the Donna dream."

Matt shook his head. "I hate to see you so upset. We finally get away from her, and she pops into your dreams. She's nothing, Kerri." He reached up and touched my cheek, and I could feel the calluses on his hand he got from playing guitar. Matt was so talented, so understanding. . . . I was beginning to feel like a total crumb for holding back the truth about tomorrow.

"Don't let Donna get to you," he said. "We're hundreds of miles away from her."

I reached up to touch his hand, nodding. He was right. And I was so wrong. How could I mislead him about what was really bothering me?

Still, I couldn't bring myself to tell him the truth . . . not yet. "I don't know why I keep thinking about her," I said, taking a deep breath. "I need to relax."

"Definitely," he agreed. "Just take all those

nasty Donna vibes and toss 'em out the window. Forever. Good-bye. End of story."

I pretended to ball up something sticky and flung it down the hall. "How's that?"

Matt grinned. "Nice try, but I think you just whacked Cami Corbis in the head."

I laughed, glancing over Matt's shoulder. That was when I noticed Jessica talking to Alex, just inside the doorway of her room. Actually, she was talking and gesturing in big-story mode, and he nodded and smiled, as if he didn't hate her anymore. How could that be?

"Hold on one second," I told Matt. "I've got to check this out."

As I wove my way over to Jessica, I noticed Maya and Erin cheering for Turtle to flip peanuts from his nose to his mouth. I leaned in close and whispered, "Looks like the ice is melting between Alex and Jess."

Maya gasped, and Erin gave me a cross-eyed look. "No way."

"Come see," I said, and they followed me over to the doorway. Jessica was telling a story about breaking the juicer when she worked at Fresh Squeezed, a juice bar at the mall.

"This sticky, gooey, oozy pulp was everywhere! In my hair, on my clothes . . . and the customer was *not* happy—to say the least."

"Jess," I interrupted, tapping her on the shoulder. "Can I borrow you for a second?" I smiled at Alex, who nodded.

"Sure!" Jess said in a booming voice.

I tugged her away, and she staggered out to the hallway with us, asking, *"Wassup?"*

"What's going on with Alex?" I asked under my breath.

"Oh, nothing, nothing!" Jess said, gesturing like an umpire who just declared a runner safe on base. "Nothing is going on. We're just having a nice conversation. *Nothing* serious. *Nothing* at all. *Nothing* to worry about."

I exchanged a glance with Maya and Erin, and the three of us broke into grins.

"Mmm-hmm." Maya said. "And you're just all giddy about the prospect of winning the wheelbarrow race in the hall."

"Are they doing that now?" Jess looked toward the door. "I told Turtle to come get me for our next heat."

She seemed to be having a great time. "As long as you're having fun," I said.

"I'm superlative. Actually, I'm really, really happy that everyone came to my party." Jessica pursed her lips thoughtfully, adding, "Okay, so I'm a little silly, but it's okay to be happy that my party was a success, right? That's good?"

"Yes," Maya said, touching Jessica's arm gently. "Happy is good."

"Good." Jess nodded firmly. "All I know is that Alex doesn't hate me anymore, and I danced with three guys, and I'm having an incredible time!"

"That's all we were looking for," Erin said, moving to the beat of the music. "Come on, party girl. Let's dance."

Jessica swung her arms wide and spun around. Erin and Maya danced toward her, closing the circle of friends.

I took it as my cue to return to Matt. Jessica was more than okay; she was having the time of her life. I was happy for her. And a little jealous. This could be a great night for me if things had worked out. Instead, I was holding back on my boyfriend and feeling like a total creep about it.

"Want to go for a walk?" Matt asked me when I found him down the hall.

"Sounds good," I said. My ears were starting to ring from the noise level. We started down the hall.

"I know a quiet place," Matt said. "How about my room?"

"What about Lloyd?" I asked, pretending to check my watch. "Shouldn't he be sleeping in the bathtub by now?"

Matt shrugged. "Believe it or not, he came to the party."

I laughed as we started down the stairs to the tenth floor. I'd been hoping for some time alone with him. It was my chance to explain things. Maybe if I said it right, he'd understand.

"We're here," Matt said, punching his key into the door.

The room was smaller than mine, but there was more of a view with a two tall buildings towering in the distance and twinkling lights everywhere.

"This is nice," I said as Matt turned off the lamp and snuck up behind me. I grabbed his arms and tugged him close. "You've been holding out on me. We should have breakfast *here.*"

"We can," he said, nuzzling my neck. "As long as you don't mind watching Lloyd eat. Not a pretty sight."

We fell back onto the bed laughing. I leaned on my elbow and studied him in the soft moonlight—his broad shoulders, his strong jaw, his beautiful, sensitive eyes. I bent down to kiss him. I couldn't resist. The touch of his lips made me shiver. There it was again, that special spark between us. Being in Matt's arms always felt so good, so right. And finally, we were really alone. A deluxe room all to ourselves. Everything would be so perfect if . . . if only I wasn't hiding something from him.

I felt deceitful, dishonest—and that wasn't like me.

I pulled away, and Matt sighed. "You have to stop stressing about Donna," he whispered. "She can't hurt you. You're with me."

"That's not it," I said. "It's something else . . . about tomorrow."

"Nervous?" He waited for my answer, but I was stuck in guilt. "That's understandable," he said.

"No, Matt. I'm nervous, but that's not it. And I feel like such a jerk about this, and I've been banging my head trying to find a way to tell you, but there's no easy way." I wrapped my hand around his, hoping he'd understand. "The thing is, I can't go to the concert with you tomorrow night." Already I could feel the tension in his hand. "The contest runs late, and I'd have to miss it to do the concert. I'm so sorry, but I never thought both things would happen on the same night."

"That's why you're acting so weird?" He sat up and stared out the window. "And you waited until *now* to tell me."

"I felt terrible about it. I knew the concert was important to you. To me too."

"But the modeling contest is *more* important," he said, a touch of annoyance in his voice.

I didn't want to argue, but the answer was obvious to me. "Well . . . don't you think it is?"

"It's just a contest, Kerri. There'll be others."

"And there'll be other jazz concerts too."

"Not with Duke Gaylord. He performs every few years, and. . . ." He shook his head. "There'll never be another concert like that. Especially for us."

I stared at him. "What do you mean by that?" Was he saying that we wouldn't be together when Duke Gaylord's next concert came around?

He stood up, still refusing to face me. "I mean, it's just a contest," he repeated. "You act as if your future as a model depends on it."

"Maybe it does," I said. "This is an awesome opportunity. If I do well, this agency is going to pick me up. And if I get some work here in Chicago, they'll pay me well. Do you know how much easier that will make my life in Miami? That I won't have to hold down twenty-five jobs while I'm in school?"

He pointed to me. "You said it. We're going off to college in just a few months. How much time do we have left together? And you want to spend it shuttling off to Chicago every weekend?"

"Not *every* weekend," I protested.

He held up his hands. "And what about us? I thought this trip was supposed to be special. Our time alone, without college pressure, without parents, without schoolwork. And what's happening? You keep running off after this modeling thing."

That stung me. It wasn't a modeling *thing*, it was my life. And I did want to spend every moment with him, but this contest was important.

Tears filled my eyes as I looked across the bed at him. I wanted to be with him. I wanted it so much that my heart was aching. But I couldn't give up this once-in-a-lifetime chance. Why couldn't he understand that? "I care about you so much," I sobbed. "But I want you to see how I feel."

"Why don't we just head back to the party," he replied. "Okay?"

"Okay," I mumbled, following him out the door, which slammed behind me. Matt was silent all the way down the hall, up the two flights of stairs.

I've got to stop this now, I thought, moving faster to catch up with him. "Matt," I called as he reached the door to the twelfth floor. "This is ridiculous. I mean, we're here together, and we're fighting. Isn't that lame?"

He shrugged. His eyes focused on the stairs.

His coldness was killing me, but I had to make him understand. "Oh, come on, Matt. Don't be mad." I gave him a weak smile.

This time he looked me in the eye. Glared at me. Before I could say anything else, he turned away and went back to the party.

Chapter 13

Jessica

"**G**o! Go! Go!" I shouted back to Turtle, who held my legs. I was paddling along on the floor as fast as I could go, but we were behind two girls from the track team. So far, this heat of wheelbarrow races was turning out to be the best.

"Time to take off," Turtle shouted. Before I could process the comment, he had lifted me around the waist and was carrying me forward. Actually, I felt more like a rocket being launched down the corridor. We pushed past the track girls and crossed the finish line first.

"Yes!" I shouted, my voice hoarse with excitement. "Yes! Yes!"

Turtle lifted me up onto his shoulders and strolled down the hall for a victory parade. Kids were clapping and cheering, as if we'd just won an Olympic medal. I was still brimming over with adrenaline as he lowered me to my feet.

"We make a great team," I said, giving him a friendly hug.

He grinned. "Anytime."

I was pushing my hair back and smoothing down my sweater when I noticed Kerri standing by the door to the stairs. "Kerri?" I shouted over the noise of the music and conversations. She looked disoriented, as if she were a stranger at the party. The minute I caught her attention, she came toward me.

"What happened?" I asked.

And she burst into tears.

I hugged her as she sobbed on my shoulder.

Maya and Erin appeared behind her. "What's up?" Erin asked.

"Damage control," I said, assuming the problem was Matt. "Let's get Kerri away from this crowd."

"Our room," Maya said, taking Kerri by the arm and leading her down the hall.

"But the party," Kerri said, sniffling. "Jessica needs to be here."

"It'll be fine without me," I said. "Besides, what could they do that they haven't already done tonight?" Already I'd seen wheelbarrow races, touch football in the hall, and the first game of Spin the Bottle since junior high.

Together the four of us marched down the hall and escaped into the quiet of Maya and Kerri's room.

"I can't believe this is happening now." Kerri lifted her hands to her eyes to wipe away the tears. "This was supposed to be a trip to bring us closer. But when I told Matt about missing the concert tomorrow night, he freaked."

I sat beside her on the bed and touched her hand. "What did he do?"

"He wouldn't talk about it. Or even look at me. He just decided to go back to the party, leaving me behind."

"That is so unfair of him." Erin pushed back a makeup bag and sat on the low dresser. "I hate guys who split before the argument is over."

I just squeezed Kerri's hand. Since they'd started seeing each other in September, Kerri and Matt had gone through their share of fights. But every time, they'd managed to work things out.

"How dense can he be?" Maya said. "He's got to see that this is a stupendous opportunity for you."

Kerri shook her head. "He doesn't. He's hurt and disappointed. I understand how he feels, but he won't even try to see my side of things."

"He'll come around," I said.

"I'm not so sure about that," Kerri said, her

eyes welling up with fresh tears. "Not this time."

"He'll get over it," I insisted. "He's going to see that the modeling contest is a great break for you. Give him some time."

Just then I heard something crash down the hall. What was that? *Probably something big and expensive,* I thought. *Probably in my room.* I shot a panicked look at Erin.

"That doesn't sound good," she said, her eyes wide with horror.

Kerri waved us off. "You guys better go see what happened."

Maya sat down on the other side of Kerri as I got up.

I felt bad for leaving Kerri, but I knew that Maya would take good care of her. I followed Erin out the door and we ran down the hall and into our room, where a few kids were gathered around the small refrigerator that had fallen onto the floor.

"Anybody hurt?" Erin asked.

"Nope," Glen said, pushing it back into the corner. "No harm done. Nothing to see. Let's all move on." He sounded like the party police. I didn't know whether to laugh or cry, but I was glad that we'd never gotten the key to the minibar inside the fridge.

I turned, only to see a couple of big-muscled

guys emerging from our bathroom, each wearing a huge white ring on one ear. Recognizing the wrestling squad, I went up to Wolfie and asked him what was going on.

He shrugged. "I dunno. But we're Lake Michigan Pirates. Like the earrings?"

"I thought it was the Pittsburgh Pirates," I said, squinting up at him. Another wrestler came out wearing a transparent silver cape. That I recognized—our shower curtain. And they were using the shower curtain rings as earrings.

"What's with the jewelry, boys?" Erin asked me.

I glanced at the wrestlers checking out their earrings in the mirror, and suddenly I just didn't care. I burst out laughing. Erin started laughing too—really laughing—and we doubled over, holding our stomachs. Right then, I felt glad to be in high school. It was as if my senior year had completely passed me by until this very minute.

For once, I was seizing the moment.

I was still laughing when Sidney Townsend came up to me and dangled her empty cup. "Got any more punch?"

"I can make some," I said, realizing the punch bowl on the dresser had only a small puddle left at the bottom. Not that I wanted to please Sidney, but I did want to keep the party going. I dropped down to my knees and reached under the bed. What happened to those cans of concentrate we stashed there? I peered under the bed and saw a face looking back from the other side.

"We found your stuff," a familiar voice said.

I straightened and looked over the bed to see who it was. Alex's head popped up. He held two juice cans. "The soda is in the bathroom. We were just going to make a new batch of punch, but I wasn't sure of the magic formula."

"I'll do it," I said, standing up.

"I'll help," he insisted.

I couldn't believe that Alex was sticking around, but I didn't question my luck. I showed him how to mix the perfect combination of juice, water, and ginger ale, since we'd run out of sherbet. "Add ice," I said. "Plenty of ice."

"Gotcha." He stirred it up with the ladle, then slid his arms around the bowl and hoisted it up. "Make way," he called to the partiers in the bedroom. "Make way for a fresh batch of Jessie James's Killer Punch."

Everyone laughed as they moved aside for Alex. He slid the bowl back onto the dresser and poured a glass. Sidney was waiting nearby to reach for it, but instead he turned and handed it to me.

I was shocked, but I tried not to let it show.

"Thanks," I said, taking a sip. I stood there for a few seconds, waiting for Alex to say something, but he didn't.

I should probably get back to Kerri, I thought as he poured himself a drink. "Well, see you—"

"You must be thrilled about tomorrow, with the class touring the *Tribune*." He turned to me.

"I am," I admitted. "It's huge compared to the *Madison Herald*." Of course, Alex knew that I was a writer. We had started off the year as coeditors of the school yearbook, until he had to fire me for being too busy with college (and Scott). Okay, I deserved it.

"Yeah, I thought of you when I saw it listed on the trip agenda," he said. "We never did rent that movie. What was it called?"

I blinked, surprised that he'd even remembered that musical. Surprised that he'd thought of me. *"Sunday in the Park with George,"* I replied. And that's when I knew that I'd always remember this class trip as the time when Alex and I became friends again.

He took another sip of his drink. "I guess you got tons of notes on the Seurat painting?"

"How'd you know?" I teased.

"Jessica Carvelli, straight-A student. It was a nice painting."

"Isn't it amazing how it's made up of dabs of different colors? The colors are like tiles on the canvas, and it takes your eye to link them together and make a picture."

"That is cool," Alex said. "But look at me, I left my notebook in the room. Oh, well, I'll just have to remember those insights if I ever need to write a paper about it. Look, if I get stuck I'll call you."

"No problem," I said. "It's the same number." Did that sound flirty? I just meant, if he really wanted help on his paper . . .

But Alex took it well. In fact, he put his cup down on the dresser and cocked his head toward the hallway. "Wanna dance?"

"Sure." I ditched my punch and followed him, worrying about what we would talk about next. We'd exhausted our supply of safe subjects, and unless Alex wanted to talk about the weather, I didn't know where this whole thing could go without becoming personal. And personal was out for us. Definitely dangerous territory.

That's the glory of dancing, I thought as we squeezed onto the unofficial dance floor in the hall, bopping in time to the beat.

The song ended, and a slow ballad came on. *Uh-oh. Romance time.* My cue to split. I looked down the hall, planning a hasty exit, but Alex reached out for my hand. "Come on, Jess," he said.

That simple. That smooth. A week ago we'd been mortal enemies, and tonight we were slow-dancing together, his body pressed against mine, his hands spread securely across my back, his cheek beside mine. It felt good to be touched by Alex, but I tried to chase that thought out of my head and file it in the "You know you've been too long without a boyfriend when . . ." part of my brain. He had a girlfriend. I was way over him. End of story.

He smelled of soap and something else sweet. His cheek felt smooth against mine. Very smooth. God, why was I thinking about Alex so much?

Because he was holding me. I turned my head slightly and there he was, his face just inches from mine. His breath was warm on my cheek and suddenly . . . suddenly he was kissing me.

Really kissing me.

Kissing me like he never did when we were a couple. Firm lips, moist mouth, tenderness . . . my mind raced back to the Truth or Dare question about who was the best kisser. I'd picked someone else, but as of this moment I'd have to change my answer. It was Alex . . . definitely Alex.

We parted, staring at each other in a daze.

Then there was an awkward moment. I felt my

palms begin to sweat as I tried to sort this out. I never thought I'd end up kissing Alex again. Not that way. It was all too confusing.

"I'm sorry," he said, his eyes so earnest.

"Really?"

He smiled. "No, I guess not. I don't know." He looked around. "Look, Jess, can we go somewhere to talk? Somewhere quiet?"

I glanced around. The party was still going strong, and the Dear Jessica side of my brain screamed that a good hostess never bails. Still, Alex wanted to talk, and I owed him that after all this time. I was sure Erin could handle things on her own.

"Okay," I said. "But my room isn't too quiet at the moment."

He took my hand and laughed, and we headed into the elevator. He let go of my hand in the elevator, but it didn't feel awkward riding down with him, crossing the hall to his room. There was a new peace between us. Friendship.

It was dark inside except for the moonlight streaming in through the window, and he didn't even move to turn on a lamp.

"It is nice and quiet down here," I said, sinking down onto the bed.

"Good," he said, "because I've been wanting to

talk to you for a while."

"Right," I said, suddenly feeling really nervous. "I'm just having a lot of trouble believing all this is happening now. I mean, do you have any idea how much I missed you in the beginning, when we first broke up? Talk about devastated." I barely gave Alex a chance to answer, but I couldn't help myself. I had to babble on. "And then, when I thought you hated me . . . how much you hated me." I groaned. "It was awful. I mean, did you really hate me?"

"I did," Alex admitted. "But only because I was hurt. It was sort of a defense mechanism."

"We were both hurt," I said. "But not anymore. We're friends now, right?"

"Right. Friends," he agreed, his eyes meeting mine. He leaned closer to me, and I blinked. He was going to kiss me.

Before I could come up with a plan, I leaned forward and kissed him back, full force. I didn't know what to think. I just knew that it felt good. Very good.

What else could I do? I decided to go for it.

"I can't believe you're actually here with me," Alex said. He leaned in for another kiss.

We had been lying on his bed, talking for hours. Talking . . . and kissing. Well, okay, maybe more kissing than talking.

I gasped when the door burst open. Joe Santini, Alex's roommate strode into the room. "Yo, Alex. How come you left the party so—" He stopped when he saw me. "Whoa. Hey, Jess."

"Hey," I replied, sitting up. And for some reason I started to feel embarrassed. I guess to the general public it probably seemed as if Alex and I were doing more than just talking and making out, which we weren't.

Joe gave a little smirk. "Well, I was just leaving," he said, and turned back to the door.

"No. Stay," I replied quickly. A little too quickly. "I mean, it's your room, right?" I added, trying to seem casual.

"You sure?" Joe glanced at Alex, who nodded. "Good," he said. Then he took a flying leap onto his bed. "Because I'm dead. About a minute later, he was snoring softly into his pillow.

Alex laughed. "I don't know how the guy does it. He falls asleep in sixty seconds flat." He leaned close to me. "I hope you're not tired," he whispered. "I don't want you to go. It's great just being with you again."

That's so incredibly sweet, I thought. How was I supposed to tell Alex I kind of wanted to leave after that? Without hurting his feelings. I glanced at Joe, who rolled over and started drooling on his pillow. "Alex . . ." I began.

"Are you thirsty?" he asked. "I'll get us some sodas, okay?"

I just nodded. And Alex was out of the room in a flash. What was I supposed to say? *Sorry, Alex. Gotta go. Now that I'm thinking about it, I'm having doubts about being in your room at all? In fact, I'm feeling more uncomfortable by the second?*

No way. I couldn't do that.

But it was true. I so didn't want to be there anymore.

What was I thinking, anyway? I wondered. I was supposed to be over Alex . . . *so* over him, after hurting so long. He had a girlfriend, and I was ready to move on. And now this . . .

I moved slowly off the bed, not wanting to wake up Joe. I didn't want to face Alex when he returned. I couldn't. I was too confused about the whole thing. I was still finger-combing my hair when I pulled open the door and shut it behind me as quietly as possible.

I rode the elevator down, wondering if other people knew that Alex and I had sneaked away. And what had we done? Danced with each other? Shared a few kisses? Definite fuel for fiery rumors.

The hall of the twelfth floor was quiet now,

though chips and cheese puffs had been smashed and ground into the carpet. Oh, well, it wasn't too incriminating. Inside I saw that Erin had straightened up the room. Sort of. Inside the bathroom, the tub looked bare without its curtain, and punch bowls were in the tub, along with a juicy red stain. Out in the bedroom, empty ice buckets were stacked against one wall in an interesting pyramid tower. Seeing that it wasn't even four-thirty yet, I decided to jump back into bed. We had hours before the class trip to the *Tribune*.

Erin turned over groggily in bed, then sat straight up when she saw me. "Is that you, Jessie James?" she asked, rubbing her eyes.

"It's me," I said, stepping out of my jeans. "Sorry I missed the cleanup. What time did the party end?"

"About a half-hour ago," Erin replied. "But forget about that. I have just two questions for you. Number one, where were you all night? And number two, what were you doing?" She rubbed her hands together in anticipation of all the juicy details.

"Brace yourself," I said, slipping my nightshirt over my head.

"I'm braced," Erin said, grinning.

"I was with Alex," I said. I saw her eyebrows

shoot up, but I shook my head. "No, nothing happened. Not like that. We did kiss, a lot. And we talked. We were honest with each other."

Erin punched her pillow and stuck it under her chin. "So this is a good development, right?"

"I'm not sure. What if I just undid months of hard work, getting over him and getting him not to hate me?"

"I'm confused," Erin said. "Let me ask you this: How do you feel about Alex right now—this very minute?"

"I don't know," I answered honestly, "and that's the problem. He's got a girlfriend. And I thought I was ready to move on. But I'll tell you this, he's definitely worked on his kissing technique."

Erin laughed, pounding her pillow in glee.

Our conversation was interrupted by someone knocking on the door.

"That's got to be Kerri or Maya checking in," I said, walking over my bed, then leaping down and landing in front of the door. I swung it open.

Ms. Gomes stared at me, her eyes furious under her bold black glasses. "So this was the party room?" she said.

I swallowed the big lump in my throat. "The party?"

Chapter 14

Before I had the good sense to swing the door closed, Ms. Gomes stepped inside and looked around. "Where did you get all those ice buckets?" she asked, grimacing.

"We collected them," I said, "but it's not what you think. I mean, they were for munchies."

She rolled her eyes. "As if that matters. I got a call from the front desk about your party. The hallway outside is trashed, the music was loud, and one student—who shall remain nameless—threw up in the tenth-floor hall outside her room. Where did you girls buy the booze?"

"We didn't!" I insisted. "We didn't buy any liquor. Maybe that kid has the stomach flu."

"Maybe," Ms. Gomes conceded. "But you did break the no-party rule. All the students were out after curfew. And you're going to be punished."

Punished. The word hit me like a ton of ice. In

the back of my mind, I'd really thought I would get away with this party thing. Wrong again.

"Since you're normally a good student—a *well-behaved* student—we won't send you home, Jessica. But there will be two weeks' detention when we return. And you will be on probation for the rest of the trip. You'll be allowed to take the tours with the other students during the day, but after dinner you are confined to your room. And no going out of the hotel during the day, except with the class. Got it?"

I nodded, swallowing hard. So this was how it felt to be a bad girl. Somehow, I didn't think I'd been missing all that much.

Ms. Gomes turned to leave, stepping around a smashed pretzel on the floor. "Oh, and Erin," she said, turning back. "Just in case you didn't realize it, you're in trouble too. Same punishment as Jessica."

The teacher walked out, closing the door behind her.

"Thanks, Ms. Gomes," Erin called cheerfully, waving at the door.

I sank down on the bed. "Oh, God. Erin, I am so sorry for getting you into—"

"Hey!" she interrupted me. "Don't worry about it. Truth of the matter is, it was worth it. Have you ever seen kids in our class mix like that? And those events in the hall. You'd think someone was giving out prize money or trophies or something."

I laughed. "Turtle was hysterical in the wheelbarrow races." I remembered our victory walk, the wrestling team with their earrings, the way the drama kids had turned my bed into a river raft and dragged the mattress down the hall. I lay back on the bed, staring at the speckled ceiling. So I'd been caught. Hadn't I still accomplished what I'd set out to do? I'd taken the dare. I'd pulled off the party. And a pretty wild one too. "You know? You're right." I smiled, thinking of the faces and laughs and jokes. "It was definitely worth it."

"Hey, everybody, a round of applause for our hero, Jessie James!" Turtle announced as I stepped onto the bus later that day. A huge cheer swelled among the students, and as I took a seat beside Erin I noticed looks of admiration from the kids around us.

"I can't believe this," I told Erin under my breath.

"Believe," she said. "You're a legend. For throwing the party and taking the rap."

"What about you?" I asked. "You were in on it too."

Erin shrugged. "I was already legendary." She

looked out the window, to the bus loading across the street. "Alex is on that bus. Glen and Kerri and Maya too. I couldn't snag them in time to let them know that we were dodging Alex."

"Thanks," I said. I had searched my soul and found no answers. I really didn't know how I felt about Alex, so I'd decided, in typical Carvelli style, to delay confrontation. "But I'm sorry you're not riding with Glen."

"We'll get over it. But how are you going to ditch Alex for this entire tour?"

"I don't know," I admitted. "And I have no idea what to say to him, either. All I've got now are more questions." Like why did it feel so right kissing him if I was completely over him? And what about his girlfriend, Suzanne? I wasn't going to steal another girl's boyfriend away. After cheating on Alex, I'd learned my lesson. Suzanne wasn't my favorite person in the world, but I wanted no part in hurting her like I'd hurt Alex back then.

When the buses arrived, I waited in my seat. Eventually, I spotted Alex standing on the sidewalk, near Kerri and Maya. I told Erin to go ahead—that I'd wait until I saw Alex go inside the building before I left the bus.

When Alex headed in, I waited another minute, then stepped off the bus and joined the rear of the crowd. I was walking into the *Tribune* building's modern lobby when I realized I was surrounded by the wrestling team. "Hey, Jessie James!" Wolfie said, pumping his fist in the air. "Jessie rocks! Jessie rocks!"

"Hey, guys, you trying to get me into even more trouble?" I noticed they were still wearing the shower curtain rings. "Nice jewelry."

"We're wearing it in your honor," Wolfie proclaimed. "You threw the party of the year." He held the elevator door open for me and pressed back to make room for me.

"I'm glad you had a good time," I said, laughing at myself. I was hanging out with the wrestling team and actually enjoying it. This was a totally new angle on senior year.

Inside the *Tribune* offices, the guide showed us the editorial department, where typewriters used to click away round the clock. Today there were only cubicles and glass-walled offices with a computer screen glowing in every one.

I didn't see Alex in the area, and assumed he'd been assigned to another tour group. Relieved, I let my mind wander back to last night. What was I thinking, going back to his room? Especially after I'd tried so hard, all those months, to get over him. And I *did* get over him. And what was *Alex* thinking? Didn't he hate me just a few days ago?

Our guide led us into the pressroom, where another group was listening. Oops. There was Alex. I ducked behind a big wrestler with a Mowhawk.

"Hey, Jessie James, what are you doing?" he asked me.

"Sorry," I said. "Just trying to avoid someone."

"Okay." He turned away from me and set his feet apart, a solid stance. "I'll block for you."

I stood there, wondering if Mohawk Boy would be willing to follow me all over Chicago. That was what it would take to avoid Alex for the rest of the trip. How did I get myself into this mess? I wished I could talk to my sister, Lisa. She always gave the best guy advice of anyone I know.

Again, I wondered what Lisa was doing in Chicago. There was only one way to solve that mystery. I would have to call her when I got back to the hotel. Maybe I could get Lisa's roommate to give me a number for Lisa in Chicago. That was, if Lisa wasn't already back in Milwaukee.

We ventured through a few other sections of the newspaper's operations. At the end we toured a room with an old printing press, then it was over. I followed the wrestlers onto the street, looking out for Alex. I saw Kerri and Maya and Luke ahead, but no Alex. Good. I hoped he was already on his bus.

"Gotcha!" Two hands squeezed my shoulders from behind, and before I even turned I knew who it was.

"Alex," I said, trying not to reveal that I was freaking inside. "Hey, hi."

"What happened?" Alex asked me, clearly concerned. "You left my room without saying anything."

"I . . . I wasn't feeling well. I'm still not," I said, only half lying. At the moment, I felt lousy.

"What is it? Stomach? Head?"

"Everything," I said, lifting a hand to my head. "Look, I've got to meet Erin. I'll catch you later."

"But, Jess—"

I couldn't help it. I just turned and ran away from him, darting onto the first bus I came to. Erin wasn't there, but Maya and Luke and Kerri were, and Kerri was sitting alone.

"Where's Matt?" I asked, falling into the empty seat beside her.

"Avoiding me," Kerri answered. "Where've you been?"

"Avoiding Alex," I said, knowing there was no way I could keep it up for the rest of the trip. I'd have to talk to him sooner or later.

Chapter 15

Kerri

"So, I'm on a boat with Donna and Matt, and the boat is sinking." I told Maya about my latest nightmare as we passed the landmark clock at State and Randolph Streets, just outside the entrance to Marshall Fields. "I keep having these dreams. Why can't I get Donna out of my head?"

"And the night before the contest," Maya said, touching my arm. "It's not fair."

"And last night there was a new twist," I said, recalling how I'd shot up in bed, shivering. "In my dream, I was handcuffed to a pole with Donna. Handcuffed to Donna on a sinking ship!"

"That's awful," Maya said. "You've got to put it behind you. Try to forget it."

"I wish I could." I rubbed my eyes, hoping the makeup people at the contest would have lots of makeup to cover the dark circles under them. "I keep telling myself that, but I can't get her out of my mind, Maya. Am I losing it, or what?"

"Hey, I've always known you were crazy," Maya teased gently as we headed toward the atrium. "But really, you're under a lot of stress. You're about to go onstage at a modeling contest in Chicago! Talk about pressure."

"Thanks for reminding me," I said as we reached the customer service area. Next to it was the line for contest registration, but I stopped walking. I wasn't ready for this yet. I wasn't emotionally prepared for what was ahead of me.

Maya frowned. "Sorry."

"It's not your fault. And the contest isn't what's stressing me out. It's Donna. And Matt. I thought I'd have his support on this," I said, my voice cracking.

Maya pulled a tissue out of her coat pocket and yanked me aside into the credit section, and we sat on a bench there while I wiped the tears from my eyes.

"Matt's an idiot for not being here," Maya said. "I'm sure he's sorry about last night. He's got to realize that it's silly to argue over a concert. But you know how guys are. It takes them weeks to articulate their feelings."

I sucked in a shaky breath, trying to pull myself together.

"Block out all this stuff that's bothering you, Kerri—both Donna and Matt."

"I keep trying," I said, "but I still see the hurt in his eyes. And this morning. Can you believe he wouldn't go near me on the newspaper tour? He can be so cold. Okay, I understand he's angry, but to totally avoid me . . ."

"Kerri, look where you are." Maya pointed to the girls in the registration line. "You're about to sign up for a modeling contest. This is just about every girl's dream come true."

"I know," I said.

"I just want you to see all that you have going for you," Maya said. "The Diamond Agency picked you to participate on their behalf. That's special. And you've got friends who will support you to the end. Even if two of them are on probation."

"I'm glad you're here," I told Maya. "We're lucky this afternoon was set aside for shopping."

Maya beamed. "Yeah, and that I did my shopping yesterday." She paused. "Are you ready, Kerri?"

I nodded. "Let's go."

When we made it to the front of the registration line, the clerk handed me a clipboard full of forms. Fortunately, I'd remembered to bring a copy of the forged permission slip, so I only had to write my name, address, and dress size a billion times or so.

After my forms were processed, the clerk directed me to another room. I stepped into the hall and nearly tripped through the doorway. A runway had already been set up. It cut through the center of the room, reminding us all why we were here. The room was lavishly decorated with swaths of sheer cloth and white flowers. The most beautiful girls I had ever seen were standing around, chatting quietly.

"What am I doing here?" I asked Maya.

She placed a firm hand on my shoulder. "Contest. Modeling. Money for school," she reminded me. "Gotta stay focused, Kerri."

"Focused, right." It sounded good in principle, but as I followed Maya to an empty seat, I couldn't help but gawk at the girls with long legs, shiny hair, big smiles, perfect bodies. Did I even have a chance? I mean, people always told me I was attractive, but I knew they meant in a natural way. The way a shiny, crisp apple is beautiful. But today I felt like an apple in a box full of sparkling cut gems.

A few other contestants streamed into the room. Then one of the contest coordinators went up to a podium and spoke into the microphone.

"I'm Sandi Perkins, and I'd like to officially welcome all the young women here to compete today. Working with Marshall Fields, we have assembled some of the best choreographers and hair and makeup artists in the business, as well as the latest in sportswear and couture. . . ."

I tried to listen, but her words seemed to float around me as I pictured Matt's face, the hurt look in his eyes when I'd told him I couldn't go to the concert. I had canceled on him twice during this trip. No wonder he was angry. Was I the worst girlfriend in the world, or what?

Someone in front started clapping, and we all joined in the applause. It felt a little fake, but I realized that judges could be watching us right now.

"In a few minutes we'll get started," Sandi went on. "You'll get your wardrobe and your makeup done, learn the choreography, rehearse on the runway, etcetera. If you have any questions along the way, feel free to ask. But for now, I'd like to wish you all the very best of luck!"

Joining the applause, I realized that everyone was standing and pushing down the aisle. I wasn't sure where to go. "What's next?" I whispered to Maya.

"You've got to go backstage," she said, as if I

was just pretending to be disoriented for laughs. She threw her arms around my shoulders and hugged me. "Good luck, Kerri. Luke and I will be out in the audience tonight. And you know Jessica and Erin will be sending you good vibes, even if they are stuck in their room."

I hugged her back, then headed to the side of the runway. A woman at the stage door checked my entrance ticket, gave me an ID card, and told me to report to wardrobe first. I found the wardrobe area—basically a bunch of racks of clothes on wheels, with a curtained-off area for trying things on. A few women, who I guessed were design people, were choosing outfits for girls.

In front of me, a girl said something about picking out her wardrobe, and a dark-haired girl from another line turned around, and corrected her gently. "That's not how they do it. The stylists pick everything."

I realized that many of these girls had been in modeling contests before. My only experience was a runway show at the mall, modeling sportswear. Listening to the other girls talk, I felt awfully small. I'd been so thrilled to do the mall show, but it was nothing compared to what these girls had been through. I tried to flash back to the confidence I'd felt at that other show, but all that I could think of was the way Donna had popped up in the audience, trying to throw me off.

Donna, Donna, Donna. Why was I obsessing over her?

As the line moved up, a tall girl with bronze hair grabbed something off one of the racks, and one of the design people lashed out at her. "What do you think you're doing? This isn't a shopping excursion, Brittany! Don't touch the clothes."

The redhead stepped back and giggled with her friend. "She doesn't have to pop a vein over it," Brittany muttered under her breath.

"She should let you pick out your own outfit," Brittany's friend said. "You have a better sense of style than the cows working here." The girl was tall and thin, and had light brown hair frosted with elegant blond streaks. She and Brittany looked glamorous already, and they hadn't gone near the professional makeup artists and stylists.

"Well, *I* know that and *you* know that, Alexa, but they know squat," Brittany said as she and her friend lapsed into giggles again. I noticed Brittany looking around to see who was watching her. The girl definitely got off on making a scene.

Suddenly she swung around and faced me, hands on her hips. "What are *you* looking at?" she asked me. When I just shrugged, she stared at me.

"Or maybe the question is, what am *I* looking at? Death warmed over? You look awful, girlfriend."

I didn't want to tangle with this chick, but I couldn't resist a sarcastic "Thanks."

"Or maybe you're just lost," Brittany said, smiling at me. "This is the modeling contest, honey. The makeovers are down at the cosmetic counter, second floor of the store."

"She'd need a heavy-duty makeover to cover those circles," Alexa said.

"But don't worry about the hair," Brittany added. "I hear stringy will be back in about twenty years."

Another girl waiting in line laughed, and I felt my stomach tighten as a handful of girls turned around to check me out. I usually wasn't at a loss to defend myself, but at the moment I was so deflated from worrying about Matt and Donna that I didn't know where to begin.

"Oh, back off, Brittany," a dark-haired girl said, stepping out of line. "Every contest you make trouble, and every contest you end up losing. Doesn't that tell you something?"

"It tells me that I'm wasting my time on these small competitions," Brittany said, folding her arms. "Though I didn't see you walking off with any prize money, Gia."

The dark-haired girl grabbed me by the elbow and pulled me into her line. "Just ignore her," she told me, pushing me in front of her. "Here . . . you're next."

Suddenly I was face-to-face with Tracy, one of the design people, who stared me up and down like the reps at the modeling agency. As she took my ID card out of my hand and taped it to her mirror, I noticed that she had dozens of rings on her fingers.

Tracy narrowed her eyes at me and reached toward the back of the rack. She pulled off a lipstick-red tie-dyed shirt with matching red cargo pants. "Try this." She handed me the shirt and pants and pointed toward the curtains.

I stepped into the changing area, a little surprised to see there were no amenities like mirrors or little dressing room chairs to throw your clothes on. Not very glamorous. Alexa was at the far end, struggling into a sleek pair of leather pants. I turned away from her and started unbuttoning my shirt.

As I changed, I wondered what Matt was doing now. What would he do about the Gaylord concert? Would he find someone else to take my ticket?

The red pants were low slung with the drawstring tied just below my navel. The tie-dyed shirt was cropped, so that a few inches of my stomach were revealed. Not really my usual style. The stylist gave me a nod of approval, then told me to change back into my clothes and go to the choreography station.

Ten minutes later I stood backstage, watching a guy named Hans put four models through the paces. "Five steps, fluid, graceful, very nice, and pause. Then pivot. Then turn back and look at the audience. Five more steps . . ."

"It looks so different from this side," Gia said, glancing out to the runway from the wings.

"Much scarier," I agreed. Gia smiled at me, and I tried to smile back, but it just wasn't happening for me. Not that I didn't want to be here, but I felt like a shadow was hanging over me.

Two other girls joined us—Brittany and her extremely thin friend. Oh, great. Nothing like learning a few steps with the nastiest models in the contest.

"Okay, next group!" Hans clapped his hands, summoning the four of us to center stage. "Welcome, ladies. There is a simple routine for you to learn. Follow along with me, please. You will take five steps out onto the runway, then pause, pivot, and turn back."

As I stepped onto the runway, I remembered the mall show. The energy of the audience. The buzz. The way Donna had sat in the front row.

Again with Donna. I wanted to grab my head and shake it till all thoughts of her turned to jelly.

"Next!" Hans ordered. "You . . . what's your name?"

I snapped out of my black fantasy just in time to realize he was talking to me. "Kerri," I answered. "Kerri Hopkins."

"Okay, Kerri, let's try it."

I swallowed. Try what? The steps? But I hadn't been listening. I turned to Gia and whispered, "What do I do?"

"Five steps, pause, pivot, turn," she whispered back without turning toward me.

I straightened, my head held high as I started forward. I tried to walk forward, looking natural and energetic. I took five steps, then stopped. What next? I turned and took a few steps back.

"No, no, no! Can't you listen?" Hans shouted.

Off in the wings, Brittany and Alexa collapsed into giggles. Gia seemed upset for me, but there was nothing she could do.

I was facing the hot opportunity every model dreamed of. And what was I doing?

Blowing it. Completely.

Chapter 16

Jessica

Drawing out my playing cards into a neat fan shape, I stared out the window of the hotel lobby as a group of kids took off, crossing the street. They were the privileged ones, the ones who had partied and escaped without punishment.

Unlike Erin and me.

Erin tucked her legs under her on the leather couch and frowned at her hand.

"Do you have a king?" Ms. Gomes asked brightly from her spot on the velvet upholstered chair.

"Go fish!" Erin said with a vengeance.

My feelings exactly. At the moment, I couldn't imagine anything more boring than playing Go Fish in the hotel lobby with the teacher who had grounded us. Why weren't we out on the town, listening to jazz, seeing a show, dancing at a club?

Oh, yeah. The big party. Our after-dinner

imprisonment. And then there was Ms. Gomes's small act of kindness. Or was it a way for her to keep her eyes on us? Not sure. But when she came up to our room with a deck of cards to "pass the time," we didn't want to insult her. Still, somehow it was worse, sitting here where we could watch our fellow students flee the hotel.

My turn. "Any twos?" I asked Erin.

"Go fish," she said through gritted teeth.

"We're all striking out here," Ms. Gomes said pleasantly. "It's up to you, Erin."

Erin didn't even glance at her card. "Got any aces?" she asked Ms. Gomes.

"Got me." The teacher slid an ace across the table to Erin. I wondered if this was the way she passed the time on a lively Saturday night at home. Go Fish and Bingo.

It was time to end the game. "Ohhhhh," I moaned and started rubbing my temples.

Ms. Gomes stared at me. "Are you okay, Jessica?"

I nodded. "It's just . . ." I winced with fake pain, then put my cards down and rubbed my temples harder. "It's just that I feel this monster headache coming on."

Erin quickly folded her cards, following my lead. "Not again." She darted a look at Ms. Gomes.

"She gets terrible headaches."

"Oh, dear." Ms. Gomes seemed concerned. "Is there anything you can take?"

"I just need rest," I said, wincing again.

"Really?" the teacher studied me suspiciously. "Heading up to your room, I take it?"

I nodded, holding my head dramatically.

"Don't worry, I'll help her upstairs," Erin said enthusiastically. Maybe a little too enthusiastically, but Ms. Gomes couldn't stop us. "Thanks for the card game, Ms. Gomes," Erin called as we moved away.

Leaning heavily on Erin, I performed a pathetic walk from the lobby to the elevator. When the doors opened, we were the only ones to step into the car. The doors slid closed, and we burst into giggles.

"I just need rest," Erin mimicked, holding her head. "A spectacular performance."

"Hey, it worked. Although now we're confined to our room." The elevator stopped on twelve, and we bolted toward our door.

"Anything to get away from that corny card game," Erin said, keying it open.

We charged inside and flopped onto our beds. "Okay, let's see what's on hotel cable tonight," Erin said, clicking the remote. "If it's Wednesday night, that means there's nothing on. Except reruns of *The X-Files*. But on what channel?"

I opened a bag of popcorn that was left over from the party. "Guess we'll have our own personal party," I said as Erin channel-surfed.

Someone banged on the door. "Party patrol," a male voice boomed through the door. "I have reason to believe you're having fun in there."

Erin hopped off the bed and opened the door for Glen. "What are you doing here?" she asked, leaning up to kiss him.

Glen grinned. "I decided to come back early and surprise the delinquent students of the senior class."

"My hero!" Erin threw her arms around him for a dramatic hug. "Come. Have some popcorn."

Glen sat on Erin's bed and tossed a piece of popcorn into the air. Like a trained seal, he caught it in his mouth.

"You must be very proud," I said.

"Hey, it took weeks to perfect that trick." Glen leaned back on the bed, and stuffed a pillow behind his head. "So Jess," he said casually, "where's Alex tonight? I just heard you two are back together."

"I am *not* back together with Alex," I insisted, bolting up on the bed. "Who told you that?"

"Heard it directly from Raffie Babkin, my

roommate. He's best friends with Alex's roommate, who says you stayed in their room last night." Glen's dark eyes were earnest. "Is that true, or just a vicious rumor?"

"Ooh!" Embarrassed, I buried my face in my hands. "It's true, but it's not the way it sounds."

"It's okay, Jess," Glen said. "We're not judging you."

"That's not it. I just got myself in this situation and I can't see a way out without really pissing Alex off. We started talking at the party last night . . . for the first time in months. Then suddenly we were dancing, and the next thing I knew we were kissing in his room. Then I fell asleep, and woke up in a panic."

"So you're not interested in getting back with him?" Glen asked.

I thought about it for a second. "I don't know," I admitted. "I don't think so. First of all, he's seeing Suzanne. But even if they broke up, I just don't know. I was over him. I was moving on. . . . And I'm wondering what's on his mind. I mean, the guy hated me for months, and now it seems like he wants to start over." I shook my head. "It's too confusing."

"Yeah, but you can't pretend you like him if you don't," Erin pointed out.

"I know, I know." I said. "I don't know what to do."

Glen smiled at me. "Nice mess you've gotten yourself into."

No kidding, I thought.

Kerri

"Pivot, turn, smile at the audience. Five steps— no! No! No! No!" Hans's words rang in my head as I changed into my sportswear selection. After he'd caught me messing up, he totally lost confidence in me. Nothing I'd done was right for him, and he'd let me know it.

Now the contest was just minutes away, and my head was full of angry faces. There was Hans, the choreographer, telling me I walked like an elephant. There was Matt, letting me know how much I'd let him down. There was Donna, viciously accusing me of stealing her boyfriend.

Why are you even here? I asked myself. In this state of mind, I didn't have a chance at winning. Not unless the judges were giving out gift certificates for psychotherapy. At the moment, I think I could beat any girl in this room for the title Miss Headcase—even Brittany with all her conniving manipulation.

I'd seen her tell a girl how great she looked, then turn around and laugh behind her back that she wouldn't be caught dead in that outfit. Girls like Brittany made it easy to believe all the nasty rumors I'd read about professional models.

"Hey, that color is great on you, Kerri," Gia said as she stepped into the dressing area.

"Thanks," I said, nervously brushing at the hem of the top.

"Don't be nervous," Gia said. "Once the show starts, everything happens really quickly."

"I'm just . . . I don't know. Lacking focus." How could I tell her what was really on my mind?

"You'll get it together when it's your turn on the runway." Gia peeled off her sweater and lifted a crocheted white top from its hanger. "And don't let Hans psyche you out. I've seen lots of girls fall apart in rehearsal and then come back to win."

"Sounds like you've done this before," I said, wishing I had her experience.

"This is my third time, and I've never even placed," she said.

"Really?" I was surprised. "You seem so confident."

"Good." Gia said. She smiled as she lifted her denim Capri pants from a hanger. "But I've been trained by the best. The Brace-Yourself-for-Brittany

School of Modeling."

I laughed, and for a moment I felt human again.

"You'd better get into hair and makeup before the contest police freak out," Gia warned me.

I touched my face. "You're right. Catch you later."

The backstage area was crowded now, and I had to weave through contestants pulling off shoes and contest reps barking orders. I passed one contestant near the door, hugging her boyfriend. That hurt. Matt should have been here for me. I wondered if he was getting ready for the concert now.

I bit my lip and climbed into a stylist's chair.

The stylist decided on a casual look to go with my outfit, and quickly combed out my blond hair and added some spray. Then I went on to the makeup station. A male makeup artist, whose nametag said August, was available.

"Have a seat, and don't move," he said, turning my head so that I faced the mirrored wall. He leaned over my head and stared at my reflection, making me feel a little nervous. "I can see someone didn't get much sleep last night," he said, going to his table to cut off a fresh sponge.

"I know," I said, rubbing my eyes, trying to

wish the dark circles away. "I look like a vampire, but—"

"Don't rub!" August's eyes widened in horror. You'd think I was sticking needles into my face. "I can take care of those circles, you silly girl. Just sit back and let me do my magic."

"Sorry," I said, closing my eyes as he rubbed some cream around them.

"You're so agreeable," he said. "The last girl I worked on didn't like anything I did." He seemed hurt.

"Was her name Brittany?" I teased.

He laughed. "Meow. It wasn't, but I have had the misfortune of dealing with the red ball of fire." He leaned down closer to my ear. "But don't you worry about her; you're in a league way above hers."

I wished that I felt that way. With all the baggage I was carrying and the mistakes I'd made today, I was beginning to wonder if my modeling dreams should have ended with that one show at the mall.

Behind me, the noise level in the room was rising, with girls laughing and talking and music sifting in from the runway area. With the contest just minutes away, I could feel the tension rising, and I was still a bundle of nerves, angry at myself for looking and feeling so awful on such an important day.

"Okay, Kerri," August applied a finishing touch of blush then stepped away so I could see my reflection in the mirror.

"Wow." I couldn't believe it. Sure, he'd concealed the dark circles and puffy eyes. But he'd also done something to make my lips look fuller, my eyes bigger and bluer, my skin healthy and glowing.

"You are amazing," I told him.

August smiled. "All in day's work." He capped a colored pencil and looked at me with pride. "But you do look great." He glanced over his shoulder to see if anyone was watching, then moved closer to whisper. "Don't mention this to the other girls, but you are gonna win this contest, Kerri."

I squinted at him. At this point the idea of winning seemed ludicrous. I was just hoping I'd be able to survive till the end. "Glad you think so," I said, as I started to get up.

August put his hands on his hips and scowled at me. "First of all, don't squint. It's hard on the eyes. Second, don't toss away a compliment, girl. Especially from someone who gives them so rarely."

I sat back in the chair. So August *didn't* make a

fuss over every model. He saw something special in me.

"I am telling you, you've got what it takes to win. You're a beautiful girl. With my help, a *gorgeous* girl. Now you just need to get out there and work that catwalk and win your prize."

Glancing back in the mirror, I felt a new hope rising. I did look good. Beautiful. Not just Kerri, the mall model, anymore. Maybe, just maybe, I had a chance.

"Thanks, August," I said. I felt a bit lighter as I stood up.

"Remember what I said," he said, wagging a finger at me.

"I will." I smiled at him with a new sense of hope.

"Kerri?" someone called. I turned toward a woman with dark hair, punctuated by a white streak. It was Jane Katz, and she was staring at me with amazement. "Oh . . . I almost didn't recognize you. Fabulous color for you, that red. Just thought I'd sneak backstage to wish you luck."

"Thanks," I said, not sure what else to say. The woman made me a little nervous.

"There's a large audience out there. But I bet you'll do well. You look great," Jane said. She was smiling now, her eyes almost twinkling.

I smiled back, sensing something really great going on. The woman who'd been so negative in her office was now beaming at me. I could see that I'd won her over. She wanted me for the agency.

Now I just had to convince everyone else out there that I was the best.

Jane checked her watch, then stepped back. "I'd better take my seat. Okay, then. Good luck." She disappeared behind a panel, and I ran to the wings to take my place beside Gia as music swelled out on the stage.

"Oh, God, this is it!" I blurted out.

"Hey!" Gia grabbed my hand. "Don't freak now. It's show time!"

But I wasn't freaked out. Excitement filled the air, and for the first time that day, I felt like I was a part of it. I was going to forget about Matt and Donna and the craziness backstage. From this moment on, I was going to step out onto that runway and start my new life.

Onstage, the emcee was talking to the audience, revving them up. Our cue song started, and the curtain swept open—our signal to line up across the stage. I stepped out, thrilled by the burst of applause.

The stage lights were warm, almost blinding. The emcee introduced the girl beside me, and I watched as she sauntered up the runway. I was next. And I was going to knock everyone out with my enthusiasm.

The model returned, and the emcee said: "Here's Kerri Hopkins. . . ."

I stepped forward for my first runway walk, remembering Hans's instructions in my head. "Five steps . . . pause." *But make it natural*, I told myself. *Smile, and show the judges that you're having fun.* And I was.

"Kerri is wearing a red tie-dyed ensemble from Hard Tail," the emcee went on. I could barely hear him, I was so wrapped up in my thoughts. *Pivot. Turn back and look at the audience. Make the movements your own. Let your body flow. Let your energy shine through.*

"The sixties may be over, but tie-dye lives on," the emcee finished as I made it back to my original mark. "Thanks, Kerri." A roar of applause rose as I flashed the audience one last smile. My heart was pounding wildly when it hit me. They were clapping for me. *For me.* And the applause was louder than before. I was sure of it.

I had made an impression.

I stepped back in line as Gia came forward for her runway walk. My thoughts raced, but I ordered myself to stay focused. I was still onstage, and there were a few more models to go.

Soon the sportswear segment was finished, and the audience clapped and cheered for all of us. We stayed onstage while the emcee introduced the judges in the front row of the audience. And then, we were signaled to head backstage into the mad rush to change wardrobe.

Moving fast, I slipped out of the red sportswear and slid on the gold silk top and lace Capri pants of my couture ensemble. Then I attached the floor-length half skirt around my waist, which allowed my pants to show. Straightening up, I felt the soft material of the shirt shift over my body. It was so comfortable . . . so glamorous. I strapped on platform sandals that were half a mile high. Clunky, but they really added to the whole long, leggy, dipped-in-gold effect.

Gia passed by in a dazzling red sequined gown. "You look killer," she told me.

I pushed my hair back over one shoulder and smiled at her in the mirror. She was right. This outfit was so perfect for me. I felt another rush of hope and energy.

"Can you hook this?" Gia asked, leaning toward me.

I fastened the hook behind her neck "That gown is beautiful on you," I said, really meaning it.

"Come on, girls," a coordinator called. "We need you all to get in place for the couture competition."

The music rose as girls scrambled onto the stage, checking themselves. I walked carefully, testing the shoes. They felt a little wobbly, but I figured I could get by with them. From across the stage, Gia gave me a thumbs-up as I took my place and smoothed my long skirt. I caught a sideways glare from Brittany, who was wearing a psychedelic shift and a large hat with a tall feather, obviously not happy with her outfit.

Then curtain opened. We were on again!

I collected myself, waiting for my turn on the runway. This was it! My big chance. And I was ready. No more obsessing about my problems. No more pity party over the fight with Matt. When the emcee called my name, I stepped forward, feeling poised and elegant. I barely needed to think about Hans's choreography as I took five steps under the light of the follow spot. Cameras flashed, but I ignored them. Instead, I focused on channeling positive energy to the judges in the first row. I glanced down into the audience with a wide smile.

One of the judges smiled back, making me feel good. I glanced at another judge, letting my eyes travel up the row.

My eyes stopped on a girl who was sitting off to the right. A girl with dark, bobbed hair and piercing blue eyes. My heart began to race when I realized who it was.

Donna!

I blinked, sure that it couldn't be true. But it was. She was calm and cool as she studied my every move.

I had to get out of there. I had to get off the stage.

I reached the edge of the catwalk as fast as I could. An explosion of flashbulbs went off somewhere in front of the runway, blinding me.

I tried to do my pivot, but I stepped on my long skirt instead, losing my balance. And before I knew it, I had landed on my butt in front of hundreds of people.

Chapter 17

The audience gasped. I could tell they felt sorry for me. Sorry because we all knew the truth: I was finished. Tears stung my eyes as the reality hit me.

Swallowing hard, I got up. I turned toward Donna for one last look, but she was gone. How could that be? How could she disappear so quickly when she was just a few yards away?

Maybe she was never really there, I told myself. *Maybe you drove yourself crazy, thinking about her so much.* I felt ridiculous. The girl was hundreds of miles away, and I was still letting her ruin my life.

"Thank you, Kerri," the emcee said. Realizing that was my cue to split, I lifted up the beautiful gold skirt and ran offstage. I felt like a total idiot.

I ran past the makeup and wardrobe stations, to the dark, empty room where we'd all stashed our clothes and belongings. I collapsed on the rug, hiding my face in my hands as I sobbed. I blew it. And I didn't even have Matt here to console me, because I blew it with him too. I was a total failure.

I didn't want to face anyone. The backstage area was quiet, but I could hear the competition still going on. The emcee called the other girls' names, and they did their runway walks. Without falling.

"Kerri?" the soft voice called.

I looked up to see Maya and Luke standing over me.

"We came backstage as soon as we saw what happened," Maya said gently. "Are you okay?"

"My ego is bruised." I lowered my chin again. "You know, I didn't just trip and fall. I lost my balance because I thought I saw Donna in the audience."

"Donna?" Maya kneeled down beside me. "What would she be doing here?"

"Exactly," I answered. "She wasn't. I'm just losing it."

Maya put her bag down and kneeled beside me. "You're under a lot of pressure," she pointed out. "And you've been having those nightmares." She pulled my hair out of my face. Then she turned her head. "Do you hear that? They're going to announce the winners." She grabbed my hand and pulled me to my feet. "Let's go backstage so we can listen."

Maya, Luke, and I went backstage and watched from the wings. The models smiled nervously as the emcee took the list from the judges' table.

"Our fifth-place winner is Carolyn Decker . . ." The audience applauded politely as Carolyn walked forward and stood in front of the other models. "In fourth place is Tara McGee!" Tara came up to stand beside Carolyn.

I knew it was hopeless, but I stood there wondering if there could be some kind of miracle. The emcee went on. "Our third-place winner is Kirsten Greenwood. And second place goes to Gia Balducci."

I smiled. At least Gia had placed this time. She'd deserved it. I gazed at Brittany, who was all smiles. I just hoped that she hadn't won.

"And first prize goes to Joy Matlock!" I turned away as Joy started jumping onstage and someone handed her a bouquet of flowers.

I was disappointed, but that wasn't the worst of it. I really was starting to think I was out of my mind. Imagining things. Having visions of Donna.

I nearly ran into Jane Katz, who'd been waiting behind me. "Kerri, I wanted to thank you for participating."

"Ms. Katz, it's not what you think," I spoke quickly, wondering if I could salvage something out of all this. "What really happened was . . . there's a girl who's been—"

"Kerri," Jane interrupted, "it's unfortunate, but I have to tell you that the Diamond Agency isn't going to take you on at this time."

I swallowed. Couldn't she at least listen to my explanation? "But can't you give me just a little leeway, since—"

"I'm afraid not," Ms. Katz said. "Our girls need supreme concentration, and I'm afraid that's a quality you don't possess."

I knew it was no use arguing with her. "Thanks anyway," I said, shaking her hand. After that, she quickly disappeared in the mob of people who were flooding into the backstage area.

"Why don't we go?" Maya suggested, scooting me back toward the room where my backpack was stored. "Do you get to keep the clothes you modeled?" she asked cheerfully.

"No," I said, feeling even more sorry for myself. I grabbed my backpack and clothes and headed over to the changing area. "I'll just be a minute." The curtained area was empty. All the girls were still out in the stage area, celebrating, con- gratulating the winners, trying to butter up agents for a fat, juicy contract. I knew that was useless for me. My modeling career was over before it really started.

All the way back to the hotel I wallowed in dark, gloomy thoughts of failure. I had let Donna upset me so much that I blew a huge opportunity. I wasn't able to focus when I needed to. By the time we walked into the hotel lobby, I could barely remember how we'd gotten there. Good thing Maya and Luke were along to take care of me.

"Let's go check in with Jessica and Erin," Maya said, pushing the elevator button. "They'll want to hear all about the contest."

"I'm not really up for that," I admitted. At the moment, reliving the entire competition would be sheer torture. "Why don't you fill them in, and I'll head up to our room."

"I'll go with you." Maya's dark eyes were full of concern. "We can hang out, just the two of us."

"No, really," I said, "I don't want to be around anyone right now. I'll probably lie down for a while. I haven't exactly been getting much sleep."

As we stepped into the elevator, Maya pressed the button for the twelfth floor and shot Luke a worried look. "Are you sure, Kerri?"

I nodded, forcing a very stiff smile.

The elevator reached our floor, and I led the

way out, determined to get some time to myself to work through the horrible feeling inside me. "I'll catch you guys a little later," I said, walking ahead.

"Okay," Maya called. "But we'll be in Jess and Erin's room if you want to talk."

I unlocked the door, ducked inside, and closed the door. At last, I was alone, with no one watching me. No one staring. No one throwing a pity party for the poor model wannabe who'd fallen flat on her butt in front of everybody.

I sat on my bed, thinking it all through again. What had really happened tonight? Was Donna there? Was it someone who looked like her? Or was I really losing my mind?

Suddenly I started shaking. It began with my knees, then worked its way up until my whole body was quivering. I hugged myself, then quickly pulled on the bedspread, but it wouldn't stop. I squeezed my eyes shut.

It's happening because you won't let the truth out, I thought. *You told Maya you were fine, but you're not.*

Jessica

"We need some noise in here," Glen said, rolling onto his back on Erin's bed. "Just because you two are on probation doesn't mean you have to stop breathing."

"Isn't it amazing that you can have forty channels but nothing to watch?" Erin clicked the remote, still surfing.

"I vote for music," I said, taking another handful of popcorn. "We've got Erin's portable CD player, but I listened to her selection all the way here on the bus."

"I've got some cool CDs." Glen sat up. "I'll go get them."

"I'll go with you," Erin said, handing me the remote. She brushed some popcorn off her jeans and headed for the door. "Be right back."

As the door closed behind them, I turned off the television and walked to the window. The moon hung over an office building in the distance, and I thought of the way the moonlight had streamed into Alex's room last night.

Alex . . . what was I going to do about him?

It didn't feel good when I blew him off outside the *Tribune* building. The guy deserved a solid answer from me. He needed to know what was going on with me. But I didn't know the answer to that myself.

I wished that some magic fairy could fly in the window and fix this whole thing for me. I thought of my sister Lisa. She didn't do magic, but she did give excellent advice. I'd called Lisa's roommate earlier to try to get Lisa's number in Chicago, but I hadn't gotten an answer.

Time to call again. If Emily didn't have the number where Lisa was staying, at least she'd know when Lisa would be back in Wisconsin. I slid my parents' calling card out of my wallet and dialed Lisa's number.

"Hello?" Emily answered.

"Emily, it's Jessica, Lisa's sister," I told her. "I'm calling about Lisa."

There was an awkward silence for a moment. "Lisa's not here right now," she said. "But if you want, I'll have her call you back when she gets in."

"Oh, I know," I said. "I know she's in Chicago. I saw her yesterday. I'm here on a class trip."

"Oh." Emily sounded confused. "Nobody tells me anything."

"I need her phone number here," I said.

"I don't have it," Emily told me. "We haven't spoken much in the last few weeks, and Lisa left in such a hurry when she dropped out."

Dropped out? I blinked, trying to process the information. "What did you just say?"

"Well, she got out of here in such a hurry that . . ." Emily's voice trailed off. "Oh, God, she didn't tell you, did she?"

I gripped the phone, scared by the growing sense of alarm in her voice. "Emily, what is going on?"

"Please, Jess, don't tell your parents," she pleaded. "You can't. I wasn't supposed to say anything. Now Lisa is going to kill me!"

I nearly dropped the phone. My sister had dropped out of college? What was Lisa *doing*?

Chapter 18

Kerri

I'm losing it. I'm really losing it.

I paced across the room, shuddering. Sleep was out of the question. My head was a jumble of thoughts.

I had lost the contest. I had lost my mind. And I was close to losing Matt.

Matt . . .

Was his concert over yet? I glanced at the clock. He might be back. I really needed to talk to him. He knew how much Donna had haunted me in the past few weeks. And my relationship with Matt was the one part of my life that I had the power to fix. The other things were beyond my control, but with Matt, there was still hope.

I pushed the bedspread off my shoulders and bolted out the door. Not wanting to wait for the elevator, I took the stairs.

When I reached Matt's floor I tugged open the

door and flew into the hallway. I was on a mission now, and it made me feel better just knowing that there was something positive I could do. Matt would forgive me. We could fix our relationship. We would make things work.

We had to.

I was halfway down the hall when Matt's door opened and someone stepped out. Matt? I wondered. No, it wasn't him.

It was Donna.

I squinted, not sure I got that one right. Donna? Coming out of Matt's room?

I reeled back, totally stunned. *So Donna really is in Chicago!* I wasn't losing my mind. Donna was at the contest.

Suddenly I stopped walking. Hold on a second. What was Donna doing in Matt's room?

Here's a sneak peek at

TURNING
seventeen #10

Reality Check
Kerri & Jessica's Story

A little bell jangled as I shoved the door open, and my sister glanced up from the cash register.

"Hi, Lisa," I said.

Lisa's brown eyes widened and she made a funny little squeak of surprise. "Jess? What are you—"

"No way," I told her. "That's my question. What are *you* doing here?"

Lisa threw a quick glance at the door behind the counter. "How did you find me?" she asked. "Was it Emily? She promised she wouldn't tell anyone!"

"Don't blame Emily," I said. "She told me by accident—probably because she didn't realize you were keeping it a secret from your own family!"

Lisa's cheeks grew rosy. "I was going to tell you, I just wasn't ready. I'm still not."

"Tell me what?" I demanded. I didn't mean to sound so angry, but I couldn't help it. I was worried and upset. "You said you were here on a road trip. Why are you working in a store? What's going on, Lisa? Are you okay?"

"I'm fine, really, Jess," she assured me.

But she didn't seem fine. Up close, she looked even worse. Her hair was dry and the ends were split. She had dark circles under her eyes. She looked like she'd lost weight too.

Could she really be taking drugs? I was afraid to come right out and ask. "Are you sure you're all right?"

She nodded. "Things are just . . . complicated."

That wasn't what I wanted to hear. "That's okay. I can understand complicated things," I said. "I'm smart, remember? Honor roll, straight A's, a special half-day college program?"

"Don't get sarcastic, Jessica."

I rolled my eyes. She sounded just like Mom, correcting my tone. "Don't avoid the issue," I snapped.

Erin cleared her throat. She was standing behind me, next to a rack of red, white, and blue shirt-dresses. "Stick to the point," she murmured.

Erin was right. Arguing wouldn't get me any answers. "I'm sorry, Lisa," I said. "I didn't come here to fight. I'm just really worried."

Before Lisa could say anything, a woman came through the door behind the counter. She had a thin face, a wide red mouth, and a stormy look in her eyes. "Oh, so you're finally here," she said. "So now I can tell you. I'm sorry, Lisa, but this isn't working."

Lisa's face turned red again. "I know I got here

late, Ms. Hamlin," she said.

Obviously, this was the boss. And she was definitely not happy with Lisa.

"Yes. Late for the third time this week," Ms. Hamlin interrupted. "I was in the office. I heard you come in—half an hour after you were supposed to be here. And now you're even upsetting the customers?"

"But, I'm not. I—"

"She didn't do anything," I piped in.

Ms. Hamlin raised her hand, not even looking at me. "I'll pay you for today, but that's it. I'd like you to gather your things and leave now."

"What? You're firing me?"

Ms. Hamlin nodded. "Like I said, it isn't working out. I need someone more reliable. I called Gina and she'll be here in ten minutes." She turned and swept back through the door.

"I don't believe this!" Lisa cried, angrily slamming the cash drawer shut. She reached under the counter and pulled out a big shoulder bag. "Just because I've been late a couple of times. It's not like people are breaking down the doors to get in and buy this nasty stuff!" Lisa slung the bag over her shoulder and sped out from behind the counter. "I am definitely out of here!"

Erin and I hurried after her as she stormed through the front door. "Lisa, slow down!" I called.

"We have to talk."

"Can't you see this isn't a good time?" she said as she hurried down the sidewalk.

"Lisa! You can't just disappear without telling me what's happening," I argued. "What are you doing here? What's wrong?"

"I keep telling you, nothing is wrong!" Lisa cried.

But she was lying, I knew she was. She always took care of herself, but now she looked awful. She was never unreliable, and now she'd been fired for being late all the time. She was my sister . . . and now she was running from me.

"What am I supposed to do?" I shouted. "What am I supposed to say to Mom and Dad?"

Lisa stopped suddenly. "Mom and Dad don't know a thing. Don't tell them, Jess, please!" she begged.

"But . . ." God, what was going on with her?

"Look, I'll call you when I'm ready to talk," Lisa declared, brushing a strand of hair from her eyes. "I promise I will. I'll explain everything. But, please, please, don't say a word to Mom and Dad!"

Before I could argue, Lisa turned and ran away from me down the sidewalk.

"Lisa, wait!" I yelled.

But she didn't even turn around.